Flight of the *Windigo*

Look for other Western & Adventure novels
byEric H. Heisner

Along to Presidio

West to Bravo (I)

Seven Fingers a' Brazos (II)

Above the Llano (III)

Del Río Hondo (IV)

T. H. Elkman

Mexico Sky

Short Western Tales: Friend of the Devil

Wings of the Pirate

Africa Tusk

Fire Angels

Cicada

Citation for Murder

Conch Republic, Island Stepping with

Hemingway

Conch Republic – II, Errol Flynn's Treasure

Conch Republic – III, Coba Libre

Follow book releases and film productions at:
<u>www.leandogproductions.com</u>

Flight of the *Windigo*

Eric H. Heisner

Illustrations by
Adeline Emmalei

Visit our website at
www.leandogproductions.com
<u>Amazon: Eric H. Heisner</u>

Illustrations by Adeline Emmalei

Cover design: Dreamscape Cover Designs
Cover photo credit: Tolga Saygin on behalf of J & T Den
Image of: Joseph Peter Green

Edited by: Story Perfect Edit – Tim Haughian

Based on the characters from HF Films - *The Windigo*

Pocket Paperback ISBN: 978-1-956417-35-7

Dedication

Film school: where dreams can be realized.

Special Thanks

Columbia College Chicago,
Amber Word Heisner, Billie Beach Jr.,
Clint Beach, & Dan Farnam

1904

In the far north, lies a land of ice and snow known only to the Ojibway. At the turn of the century, word of this place and its supposed riches has spread. American expansionism into the West has reached its end.

The northern frontier and its spoils are there for the taking, only to be protected by…
The Windigo

I

The thunderous roar of an engine breaks the silence over a snow-covered wilderness. Not a conventional-looking craft, this innovative flying machine, based on the 1842 designs of William S. Henson and powered by steam, bridges the gap between Leonardo da Vinci's primitive gliders and engine-powered flight. With a one-hundred and fifty-foot wingspan, the silk-skinned, wood-frame airplane soars, with curved, bat-like wings, several hundred feet above the landscape. A plume of smoke, from the coal-fired boiler pipes positioned mid-ship, trails-off behind them.

Sporting a leather, aviator cap with goggles, Clarence "Wings" Walker maneuvers the controls from the rear position of the two-seat airplane. He peers out the side of the bulky cockpit, and studies the ground as it passes below. Light-footed on the rudder controls, Wings eases off the throttle and lets the aircraft descend in a slow, arcing turn.

He reaches ahead to the forward seat, taps his copilot on the shoulder, and then points to a frozen lake in the distance. Samuel "Pooch" Malone sits with a waxed-paper topography chart spread out over his lap and carefully plots their position and intended route. He recalculates their location on the map, turns with two gloved fingers held up, and points ahead. Pulling up from the descending arc, Wings steers to the north, and the steam-powered aircraft slowly fades into the wintery, grey sky above the horizon.

~*~

A pair of pack-laden figures, in animal-hide overcoats, snowshoe across a frozen lake surrounded by woodland. Leading, Quaid heaves warm breaths through frozen whiskers. He licks the icicles that form on his hanging moustache and smooths his gloved hand over his beard. Squinting his eyes to protect them from the glare of the snow, he glances behind at his Indian wife following, and trudges onward.

In the face of a strong wind, Quaid stops to cautiously look around. The area appears uninhabited, except for an unusual set of tracks crossing the lake, plowed deep and perpendicular to their own. Snowshoes crunching on icy snow, Quaid cuts across the unfamiliar trail and continues his trek. After plodding several paces, he stops, and then looks back. Behind him, the woman stands stock-still, frozen with fear.

Wisps of shallow breath escape through cold, blue lips, as her wide-eyed gaze lingers on the strange set of tracks. Snowshoes deep in a drift, pointed forward, Quaid pivots at the waist to wave her onward. The native woman stares at him, vigorously shakes her head for a moment, then remains still. Taking exaggerated steps to turn, Quaid moves toward her.

Promptly, she backpedals in an overwhelming fear, as if she is about to meet the devil himself. Stumbling with her pack, she lands hard on her backside. In a flurry of ice and snow, Quaid rushes at her. He grabs hold of the panicked woman, pulls her up, and gives her a violent shake to return her to her senses.

Her terrified scream shoots through the trees and is lost in the howling wind.

Her attempt to twist from his firm grip is matched by his urge to restrain her. Quaid stares at the frightened woman, puzzled by her sudden change of heart. Finally, he manages to pull her along behind him, as her chilled breath utters a prayer, and her eyes fill with tears of dread.

~*~

In a mountain cabin, tucked far away from civilization, a group of hardy men in heavy winter clothing surround a flickering woodstove. As snow falls outside, the men warm themselves, occasionally glancing through the glass window. Across the room, a broad-shouldered Native American stares beyond the frosty windowpane into the bleakness of winter. Suddenly, he feels a cold chill of trepidation, and he glances at the group of men illuminated by the glow of the stove. In a low, somber tone, so the others won't hear, he murmurs an inaudible chant. Then, he mutters, "'Tis a *Windigo*..."

Outside, the icy winds of an approaching storm howl through the trees and whip fiercely against the cabin.

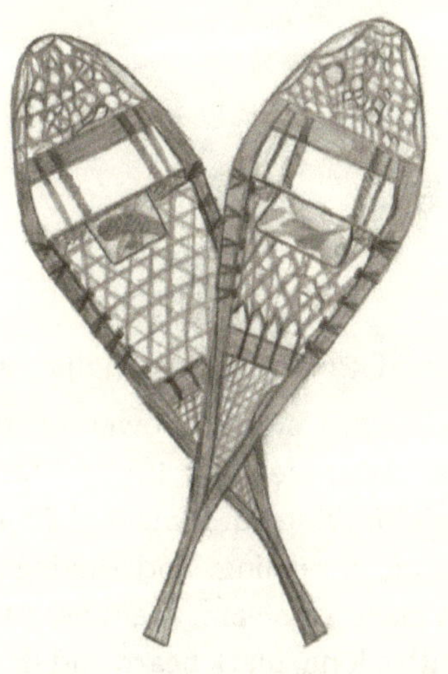

II

Attached to a massive engine, a growling boiler belches steam, powering valves and pistons. As it devours timber, this piece of industrial milling equipment creates a melody of ripping, thrashing, and sawing. Emerging from a haze of steam, Hammer, a heavy-set man with a long, black beard and the look of an engineering blacksmith, bares his teeth in a satisfied grin. He tosses an oversized monkey wrench to the side, wipes his hands on his leather apron and lifts his mechanic goggles from over his eyes to his forehead. "Dat should do it."

He struts over to a nearby drafting table, where a bespectacled female, dressed in a woolen suit, studies charts and blueprints. Charlotte Evans pencils in numbers, looks up at Hammer and then moves a page aside to reveal the header on the plans: *S. P. E. C.* *(Steam Powered Engineering Company)* She nods her head in confirmation and yells to him over the thrashing sound of the steam-powered machine. "The master cylinder should be functioning at maximum velocity for the rigger aperture to allow for cohesion."

"Yep…" Hammer wipes his grease-stained hand across his mouth, tugs on his beard and then drags a finger across the blueprint. "Da adjustment was here… and also here."

Staring across the table at the goliath of a man, Evans pushes her wire glasses higher up on her nose and comments, "Did you adjust for sway?"

"Yep…"

Pleased, she straightens up in her seat and smiles at him. Both turn to the monstrous machine with its boilers, gauges, and coils of brass tubing surrounded by hissing clouds of mist. "Well, then… Our work here is concluded."

Hammer rubs his dirty chin whiskers, smiles and nods. "Ya, dat should do it."

~*~

A tent-city logging camp is surrounded by felled trees, empty wagons, and recently abandoned forestry equipment. Canvas on the frames of temporary buildings flaps in the breeze, accenting the eerie emptiness of the site. The camp, which once supported dozens of industrious workers, now stands with not a soul to be seen.

Snow crunches underfoot, as Quaid steps out from the surrounding woods and pauses to look the abandoned camp over before entering it. Warily, he gazes around before looking back to the woman reluctantly following. "Come 'ere, gal…"

Smelling something foul in the air, her body tenses up. Her eyes go wide, and she gives a deliberate shake of her head. "*No…!*"

Quaid frowns. He sets his rifle against a tree stump, drops his backpack on the ground and turns to address her. "Enough a'yer crazy nonsense, woman! Let's make camp here. Git a fire goin', 'nd cook us somethin' to eat."

After removing his snowshoes, Quaid grabs his rifle and explores the vast logging operation further. His gun held ready, he peers into numerous tents to find them still set up with equipment and supplies. Nearly everywhere he goes, a strange, foul stench lingers in the air. When he pauses to study some unusual tracks in the snow, a peculiar feeling passes over him. He mutters, "That's odd..."

~*~

In the trading post cabin, the men gather at the makeshift bar for drinks and to hear a recently arrived man speak of news. Fenimore Cooper is a fur-trapper of French, Irish, and German descent. He has traveled extensively across the northern frontier, living and working in harmony with the local tribes. The owner of the establishment sets a cup before him and asks, "How's it look up north, Fenimore?"

The trapper lifts the clay vessel, takes a lengthy swallow and then shakes his head. "No good..."

A man, dressed in the furred garb of a buffalo hunter, leans toward him. "Why haven't we heard from the others?"

Fenimore has another drink, stands silently looking at each one of them and finally answers. In a low, mysterious tone, he says, "There is an evil spirit about. It travels on the wind..."

Unsettled, one of the men steps forward and speaks. "They will soon need to come back here for supplies."

Coldly, the trapper looks directly at the man and utters, "They will *not* be coming back."

III

In the slanted light of the winter sun, Quaid sits fireside, smoking a long-stemmed, clay pipe. Spread out before him lies the abandoned logging camp. Pondering the unusual situation, he studies everything. He stares long and hard. Finally, glancing over to his wife, he lets a puff of smoke escape his lips.

Squatted beside the cook-fire, the woman prepares food. A noticeable tremble in her hands increases, every time a gust of wind passes. She constantly sniffs the air while trying to calm the terror inside her. Suddenly, she bolts upright, looks around and then listens

Flight of the Windigo

intently to a rumbling noise in the distance. Everything becomes quiet and her eyes widen in a display of overwhelming fright. The sound suddenly returns at a roar, and the steam aircraft emerges above the trees and flies over. The sight of the flying machine is too much for the primitive woman to comprehend, and her mind snaps.

Quaid stands, as she lets out a blood-curdling scream and dashes into the woods. "Woman…! Git back here!" Looking to the sky, his gaze follows the smokey trail of the airplane as it circles around once, dives lower, and then swoops in for a landing beyond the trees. He does a quick double take, when he notices something else in the treetops, but his attention is diverted again by the continuing screeches of the woman. "Gol-dammit…! What *is* it that's got that durned woman scared out of her gourd?!?" After strapping on his ammunition belt, Quaid picks up his rifle, kicks out the campfire and walks toward the location where he last spotted the flying machine through the trees.

~*~

In a clearing, the steam-powered flying machine's propeller spins to a halt. Wings and Pooch climb out and take a moment to find their equilibrium after the extended flight.

Wings takes off his leather helmet, slings it into the cockpit and looks around. "Are you sure this is the place, Pooch?"

Folding up the big topography chart he was studying, the navigator nods his head. "That's what it says on the map. This cut in the wood was put here for the freight wagons to turn around during the summertime months." Snow crunches as Wings steps away from the airplane and gazes out to the dark shadows along the tree line. "Strange there isn't any work going on, or anyone here to meet us… It's awful quiet."

Stepping around the aircraft, Pooch sees only snow, sky, and trees. "I guess that's why they wanted us to check it out…"

Wings shoots his copilot a sarcastic look. "*I guess* so… Let's check it out then, shall we?" He walks to the aircraft, reaches into the cockpit and pulls out a Winchester rifle. Looking once again at the thick, foreboding forest, he levers the action to put a round in the chamber and proceeds toward a path that has been cut through the trees.

~*~

Arriving at the abandoned logging site, Wings and Pooch examine some left-behind gear and forestry equipment. As he looks

14

around at the canvas, Wings toes a rusty axe blade. "This is the place, alright…"

Pooch peeks inside one of the tents and then lets the door flap fall closed. "It looks like everything is in working order."

"Yeah… Just, not *working*…"

The navigator walks down the row of tents and, at the hint of smoke, pauses to sniff the air. "Where *is* everyone? Smells like something cooking…"

The nearby sound of a rifle cocking breaks the silence. Wings and Pooch turn to see Quaid step out from behind a tree. Cradling the rifle casually across his arm, the long-bearded frontiersman tilts his head. "Who're ya lookin' fer, 'xactly?"

Pooch suspiciously eyes the man's rifle and fur coat, then blurts, "Who the hell are *you*?"

Quaid shifts the position of his gun, so that the muzzle points in their direction. "I was here first. You's the ones who come sailin' down from the sky."

Keeping the barrel of his rifle pointed at the ground, Wings moves toward Quaid. "We aren't looking for a fight." He uncocks his Winchester and holds it non-threateningly. "We're contracted by Kishwaukee Valley Logging & Supply. All progress reports from this camp ceased a few weeks ago, and we were sent up here to investigate."

Quaid looks around at the uninhabited logging camp. "No progress, 'cause nobody's here. Found it a mite peculiar."

Watchful, Pooch keeps back and repeats their mission. "We were sent up here to find out what the situation is."

Wings nods and adds, "How long have you been here? Have you seen or talked with anyone?"

Quaid lowers his rifle and waves them over, muttering, "Come on o'er to my bivouac. Yer arrival interrupted my meal 'n run off my woman"

They watch him amble off before exchanging a wary look and following. Pooch whispers aside to Wings. "It looks like they didn't hardly pack anything and took off in a hurry."

The hunter peers over his shoulder at them and grunts, "They didn't pick up 'nd go... They jest got gone."

Confused, Wings looks at Quaid. "How do you mean?"

Quaid stops and turns to them. He looks around the empty camp and waves an arm at the vacant tents. "When this many folks leave a place all at once, there's a trail."

Flight of the Windigo

Standing in the middle of the camp, Wings looks out to the dense, surrounding forest. "Which way did they go?"

"*Nowhere* is where they got."

Surprised, Pooch glances around. "How's that?"

Quaid points down the main avenue through the tents to a cut in the trees, and then turns to another path that leads out to the clearing. "There are only a few trails cut into this area. One to the south, and the one to where you two come in…"

Wings queries, "They went south?"

Quaid shakes his head. "If they did, there weren't no tracks t'be found."

Wings skims the toe of his boot over the fresh snow. "Are you sure?" He walks to the edge of camp and looks at the untrod snow. "Maybe the weather covered their tracks?"

Slowly shaking his head, Quaid replies. "Not a one, animal or otherwise, has come in or out of this place fer days. 'Cept fer you 'nd me…" As the breeze blows his hair and prickles his neck, he looks over his shoulder to the trees. "Nothin's that leaves a track bin through here that I can tell."

Unsettled by this news, Pooch steps over beside Wings. "Well, where *is* everyone?"

Speaking in an eerie tone, Quaid starts to walk away. "Like I said… They're jest *gone*."

The pair follows Quaid, and Wings calls ahead when they get to the far end of the camp. "*Why…?*"

The frontiersman stops, thinks a moment, then shrugs his shoulders, scratches his beard and lets out a heavy sigh. Turning to face the pair of visitors, he is about to speak, when, with a heavy thud, a frozen boot suddenly drops from above. Aghast, the three stare at the bone of a half-eaten leg poking out from inside the boot. In unison, they slowly look upward to see a virtual meat locker of bodies hanging in the high reaches of the tree canopy. Pooch promptly twists to the side and vomits. As a sickening fear wells up inside them, Wings and Quaid pull their gaze from the gruesome sight and lock eyes on each other.

IV

Wings is the first to break the silence. "Who could do this?"

Resisting the urge to look up at the suspended bodies, Quaid warily peers around the camp. Defensive, he utters, "You's the ones who come down from the sky... *You* tell *me!*"

Pooch spits the taste of vomit from his mouth and gives Quaid a suspicious look. "*You* were here when we arrived..."

Looking down at the severed leg, the mountain man shakes his head. "This wasn't the work of *any* man..."

~*~

At a conference table in the Kishwaukee Valley Logging & Supply Company headquarters, several businessmen sit gazing at charts pinned-up on a wall. One of the wool-suited executives steps up. Using a pointer stick, he indicates large regions along the top portion of a map. "We've been having problems with communications on the northernmost frontier. A week ago, we sent up a scouting crew to find out what's been happening there."

"Have we received their reports?"

The executive glances at a stack of papers on the table, takes a deep breath and then swallows. "Nothing promising… What information we *have* received is minimal. The report states that operations have been abandoned by all personnel."

Everyone in the room is astonished at this news, apart from the man standing before the charts and one of the gentlemen seated at the table, Jim Burrows. While the others shuffle the papers in front of them, Burrows stares down, studying the wood grain of the table and avoiding the questioning stares of his associates. One of the investors clears his throat, gazes around the table and then asks the obvious. "You say *abandoned*…? Where did they go?"

Keeping his composure, the executive standing before the map replies. "Our guess is that, with cold weather coming, they moved south."

"Everyone…?"

"It appears that way."

"What about all the equipment and supplies?"

"The report states that everything is still there."

"With no one to do the work…?"

"The information we have received thus far is peculiar. We believe the natives of the area might have scared them off, or perhaps a competing logging operation came in and poached our workers with promises of better payment and benefits." Scanning the men seated at the table, the executive receives stares of disbelief. "The objective of this meeting is to determine if we are to continue operations on the northern frontier or pursue other avenues of revenue."

Examining several spreadsheets of figures, one of the investors pipes in. "The resources there are *unmatched.*"

Another scans his copy of the financial report and speaks tersely. "Can't we just hire another crew?"

After the executive and Burrows lock eyes momentarily, the presenter clears his throat to speak. "I was hoping you gentlemen would suggest that option..." Burrows offers a nod, picks up his pen and scrawls something down on the report in front of him.

~*~

Wagons are heavily laden with supplies for the cutting crew, along with steam-powered machines for milling. Supervising the loading of equipment, Hammer inspects each wagon before checking it off on the inventory. Seated nearby, Evans flips through the overstuffed file folder open on her lap. She scans some reports, turns to find Hammer and calls to him, "The resources in the area are estimated to be as plentiful as one thousand per foot by acre."

Hammer checks a rope fastened over a tarped wagon. "Yaugh... Is dat goot?"

"That is very, *very* good."

"Well, dat's why dey're sending us up dere den."

She glances up from the reports and shakes her head. "No... They're sending us, because the last crew mysteriously disappeared without a trace."

Hammer tightens a knot and glances over his shoulder. "Dey took off for da winter?"

"Nope... Just disappeared..."

He turns to see if she is joking with him. "Dat's funny..."

"Not really... The reports they gave us are a bit vague as to what actually happened. Only that there were no tracks in or out of the camp... Nothing to follow up with."

Hammer shrugs and goes back to securing the load. "Dey prob'ly missed deir trail somewhere in da woods."

"They surveyed the whole area by air. Nothing found... No trails, no loggers... Only the camp was left behind."

Hammer turns to her and smiles. "Maybe, someday, we'll be able to git all *dis* stuff into da woodlands by air!"

Nodding her head, she looks back to her files and charts. "By that time, there probably won't be any virgin forest or trees left to harvest."

He grunts in agreement and mutters under his breath. "Whatever happent to dem is no matter to me. A job is a job."

"What if the situation there makes this job the last?"

"You mean, I could retire?"

Dubious, Evans laughs, tilts her head at him and states. "Or, *be* retired... Something very peculiar happened up there. The *powers-that-be* expressed that our preparation funds for this are *nearly limitless*."

Flight of the Windigo

Hammer pats the brand new sidearm strapped to his leg. "I know! Ain't it swell to have dem foot da bill for a few extras?"

"I think it's very suspicious…"

The big man leans on a wagon wheel and turns to her. "You don't have to make it on dis trip. I can set up da operation, and you can come along with da first wave of supplies."

Coldly, she stares at him. "I'm *going* as planned…"

"Yeah…?"

"Yeah."

"Dat's a good gal, Evans… Always knew you were cut from a different cloth."

"What's that mean?"

"Well, most ladies are more of a silk or a fine cotton."

"Yeah…? And, what am *I?*"

"Burlap…" At the back of the wagon, Hammer lifts the corner of the tarp to reveal the shiny receiver of a machine gun tucked in with the equipment. "I tought it was strange, as well, and procured an extra measure of protection, just to be cautious. I'm bringing dis along, in case we need it in da field."

Evan's eyes light up at the sight of the weapon. "Wowzers! Will you let me shoot it?"

"You bet I will!"

"Thanks, Hammer! The incredible engineering of those things has always fascinated me."

Grinning through his shaggy moustache, he grunts, "Like I said b'fore, you's a bit different dan most udders…" Smiling back at him, she shrugs demurely and goes back to studying her reports.

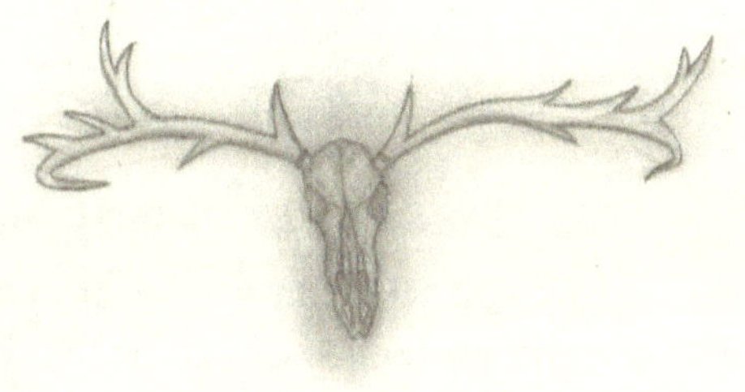

V

Snow falls gently on the frozen landscape. Tree limbs creak with the weight of clinging ice, and a stiff breeze loosens chips that break free and clatter to the ground. Tied alongside the frontier trading post, a saddled horse and two pack animals patiently wait, as smoke rolls out from both a stone fireplace chimney and the exhaust pipe of a stove.

Quaid warms himself at the hearth of the crackling fireplace, as he looks at the grim faces around him in the room. His searching gaze comes to rest on Fenimore, and he asks, "Those yer pack animals tied outside?" The trapper nods once, but doesn't utter a word. He maintains eye contact with Quaid and then, looks away. Scanning the others, Quaid continues. "Them fellas was way up high, danglin' in the trees. Was like some animal… or *thing*, hung 'em up there. Like we would do, as food storage fer the winter…"

One of the bearded men scratches his cheek and asks, "They was all *dead*…?"

Quaid looks to him and eerily replies, "*Worse* than that… Some of 'em was half-eaten. Or, jest nibbled on… I never seen no sorta creature that would do such a thing."

One man murmurs, "Maybe bears…?" Another hunter nods in agreement.

After taking out his pipe, packing it with tobacco and lighting it, Quaid blows out a puff of smoke. He looks at the man and shakes his head. "Weren't no bears… There was over a dozen fellas in 'em trees. Jest hangin' there like human fruit." Standing back in the shadows, Fenimore looks at the native woman in the corner. Seeing that she is out of her mind with fear, he unconsciously puts his hand to the handle of his knife.

Then, a logger chimes in. "Some Injun tribe could've done it to scare us out of the territory!"

Quaid puffs on his pipe again and eyes the whole group. "No native I heard tell of would do such a thing. Much less not leave a tell-tale mark of some sort… Whatever done it has one helluva devil-like disposition."

The logger retorts. "There are tribes up here that no one knows about. People hidden from civilization…"

Quaid takes a drag from his pipe and ponders a moment. "Maybe so… The loggin' comp'ny footin' the bill sent up some scouts by air to check the site. After we found the dead bodies, they were off agin, quick. I'd wager that the up-high view of them damned corpses was even more horrid on their way out. That one poor fella prob'bly still ain't eatin' solid foods yet." Quaid looks at Fenimore again, sucks at the stem of his pipe and then taps the clay bowl on the stone fireplace. "Whoever, or *whatever*, it is… They murdered *ever' one* of 'em." His eyes dart to his wife shaking in the corner, and then he continues. "Not a soul remains to tell the tale… We buried what we could in the frozen ground, but there was so many up in them trees, we weren't quite up to the task."

Shocked, one of the horrified lumbermen grumbles, "*You didn't git 'em all down?!?*"

"Hell, the only way to git to some of 'em was to cut down the whole tree. I'll leave *that* sort of work to *yer* kind."

Flight of the Windigo

As a murmur spreads through the room, another logger speaks up. "What creature would *do* such a thing?"

One of them exclaims, *"The murderin' bastards…!"*

The lumberjack turns to look at him. "Who do *you* think done it?"

"It was prob'ly one of them competin' loggin' outfits. They don't like independents, and they're tryin' to scare us off."

While listening to the general discontent and accusations, Quaid calmly puffs on his pipe. Then, he adds, "Well, they sure sent a message that they don't plan to tolerate you folks bein' 'round…"

Fenimore unobtrusively emerges from the shadows and steps through the crowd. The chatter in the room falls quiet, as he clears his throat and then speaks in a low tone. "It is not human or earthly beast that did this. 'Tis the work of *Windigo*… This is the valley of the Windigo. Its path has been crossed. And, it has been awakened." The people in the room look at each other. Some of them don't know what to think about Fenimore's strange tale, and many are outright skeptical.

Suddenly, a blood-curdling cry erupts from the woman huddled in the corner. Surprised, everyone turns to see her lunge and grab hold of the man nearest to her. Her shrieks merge with the man's own terrified scream, as she claws at his eyes and bites off his nose. Several of the men leap into the melee and rip her from the bloody victim. They forcefully pin her down to the floor and restrain her from attacking further. Bellowing through blood-drenched fingers clamped over his face, the man cries out, "*She's bit off me nose!!!*"

A burly lumberjack presses his hand against her head to stop her from twisting away and tries to pinch the severed cartilage from her teeth. "It's still in her mouth!"

Another man tries to pull the piece of nose out. "Hold'er, and I'll get it..." She gulps it down and clamps her jaws onto his finger. "*Yeoooowww!!!* She's *got me*, dammit!"

With his free hand, he repeatedly smashes his fist against the side of her face, until he can remove his injured finger from her mouth. "What's the hell's *wrong* with her?" Holding his chomped finger, he picks a stray tooth from the bloody wound. "She's like a rabid wolverine!" He looks over to where the first attack victim whimpers pathetically while holding the bleeding cavity where his nose once was.

Carrying a wooden club, the owner of the trading post comes around the bar to stand

Flight of the Windigo

where the shrieking woman struggles to get free. He quiets her with several good conks on the skull and then points outside. "Chain her in the woods! Away from the dogs…"

Observing the frightful episode from his seat by the fire, Quaid places his still smoking pipe into his coat pocket. Watching in disbelief, he mutters, *"What devil got into her…?"*

Despite the frenzy of activity, Fenimore remains stoic. With a knowing expression, he replies, "She is *Windigo*."

~*~

A train of supply wagons pulled by draft horses travels northbound through the snowy wilderness. One of the wagons carries parts of a steam-powered sawmill strapped to its bed, while the one following has the boiler, with its multiple gauges and protruding lines of copper tubing. The others have canvas tarps stretched over various sized wooden crates and barrels. Beneath the canvas coverings, the containers are stenciled with the letters: *S. P. E. C.*

Rotating with those who get to ride in the last wagon, a group trudges along the trail cut through the snow by the animal teams and wagon wheels. Leading them, Hammer is armed with a pistol and knife on his belt, another gun in a shoulder holster, and holds a sawed-off shotgun. He looks to his small-statured partner, Evans, and asks, "D'ya tink we shoult have brought more guns?"

She looks behind at the army of heavily armed loggers and engineers following. "I think maybe we should have brought more folks that would know how to use them."

Hammer looks back at the various strong, lumberjack-types and the more formally attired engineers. Glancing down at the gun cradled on his arm, he flashes a grin. "Da show of weaponry is what's important. We shoult be able to scare away both da competition or any ne'er-do-well natives."

Evans grimaces at his logic and looks to the trail ahead. "Just don't start shooting anything. With this group of timber-brutes and brain-busters, *we're* more likely to get riddled with bullets than the other fellas."

As his grin broadens, Hammer leans over and whispers to Evans. "I only gave ammunition to half of dem."

Astonished, she turns to him and asks, "Which half...?"

"Da ones who knew how to load it."

"You mean, half of them *didn't*?"

Hammer gives an acknowledging nod to her blatant show of surprise. "You'd be some shocked."

S.P.E.C.

VI

The steam aircraft is northbound over a canopy of frozen trees. Wings, at the controls, reaches forward to tap Pooch on the shoulder. He hollers above the engine noise. "How far yet?"

The navigator looks up from the charts on his lap, adjusts his goggles against the frigid air and yells back to him. "About an hour to go before we reach the frozen lake!"

Wings jabs a finger at the dark, stormy sky ahead. "Looks like we might be in for some bad weather!"

Flight of the Windigo

Pooch gives him an affirmative gesture and yells back, "We should arrive before we reach that!" With a nod, Wings ducks low in the breezy cockpit and returns to his pilot duties.

The dark clouds increase. Exploding over the treetops and across the frozen landscape, the ghastly screech of an unnatural being rapidly spreads. The snowstorm slams and tosses the aircraft. Its wing struts and tie cables nearly snap from the strain. Blinded by the weather, Wings and Pooch hold tight, as they try to find a place to land. As trees rip past them, mere inches below the rocking wingtips, Wings fights at the controls, barely keeping the canvas structure aloft.

With his navigational maps tucked-in between his seat and his leg, Pooch scrunches low. He peers out past the front of the airplane and can see nothing but white sky and bursts of blowing snow. Suddenly, a cracking of the frame is followed by the ripping sound of canvas, as the aircraft rapidly loses its lift. Wings struggles desperately with the controls and yells, "Dammit! We broke a strut! *Hold on!!!*"

Pooch pushes himself deeper into the wicker seat and stares, wide-eyed, as the airplane skips across the icy treetops. Then, in a blinding flurry of snow and cracking tree branches, the craft tears past the forest canopy and tumbles to a clearing at the edge of the frozen lake.

~*~

A winter storm howls fiercely outside the trading post. Sled dogs cower and brace themselves against gusts of snow, and pack animals put their hindquarters to the prevailing wind. Chained to a tree trunk, the native woman tugs at her restraints. Her agonizing screeches add menace to the frightful storm, spooking the horses until the hitch line rips from the building. Tearing their halters free, the animals dash away into the storm.

Blasts of icy wind rattle the wavy glass windowpanes of the trading post, and blow down through the chimney, flickering the firelight and spreading ash across the floor. Silently, Fenimore stands watching the blizzard rage outside. Standing at the bar, the others in the room drink home-brewed liquor to both warm themselves and settle their rattled nerves. Listening to screams of the woman outside, one of the burly loggers shakes his head and mutters, "For heaven's sake, I wish she would stop carryin' on like that!"

Flight of the Windigo

Several lift their tin cups in agreement. One of them finishes his drink and turns to look outside. "Maybe we should bring her back in?"

The man with the mauled finger taps his bandaged stump on the bar and nods to the nose-less one across the room. "Ya dare bring that lunatic back in here, I'm leavin'!"

Holding a long-barreled game rifle, a hunter at the end of the counter grunts, "Soon as this storm plays out, I'm gettin' the hell away from 'ere." They all nod in agreement, as the trading post owner opens a fresh jug and pours another round. From the far side of the room, a muffled chant grows in volume, and they turn to where Fenimore stands before the window. The man with the gun taps the butt of his rifle on the floorboards and grimly mutters, "Ya got somethin' more to say over there, Frenchie?"

Staring at his reflection in the curvy window glass, Fenimore pauses his chanting to speak in an eery, low whisper. "It is *coming* for us… No one escapes the *Windigo*."

The hunter lifts his rifle and holds it against his chest. "Hell, I ain't never seen a Windigo, but there's no sort of animal I heard of that cain't be hunted."

Glancing back at the counter lined with outdoorsmen, Fenimore pauses, slowly shakes his head and gravely repeats, "*No one* escapes the Windigo…"

One of the men slams his drink down and hollers, "Dammit, Fenimore…! If you spout that old-wife's tale one more time, I'll shoot you myself and feed you to the dogs!"

The trapper turns back to stare out the window, while the others grumble amongst themselves. As the tormented shrieks of the woman outside continue, the tavern owner thumps the jug of whiskey on the bar. "Easy there, fellas… Ain't no need for us to go turnin' on each other."

Sitting near the fireplace, Quaid's shadowed features momentarily light up, as he strikes a match and puts it to the bowl of his pipe. "Yaugh, that's prob'ly jest what it wants…" Everyone's attention shifts to Quaid, illuminated by the firelight behind him, as he puffs out a cloud of smoke.

A lumberjack, holding his refilled cup, nervously asks, "What *who* wants…?"

Quaid casually motions over to Fenimore at the window with the stem of his clay pipe, and another man warily answers, "The winter beast he speaks of…?"

Raking his fingers through his whiskers, then clenching the pipe in his teeth, Quaid takes several puffs and nods. "Whomever…or *whatever* it might be… Fear of the unknown is a crafty weapon. It can immobilize an army or make the few in number overcome the masses. The way I see it, we need to stick together to fight *whatever* it is, if we're to survive."

Clinking tin cups with the neck of his home-brew jug, the tavern owner tops-up more drinks. "He's prob'ly right. Everyone should jest stick close by here till it all passes."

A lumberjack looks to his cup and then to the supply of jugs against the wall behind the bar. "That's fine for you sellin' us yer wares. I have ta find me another job."

As a trickle of smoke escapes his lips, filtering through his overhanging moustache, Quaid grimly mutters, "I know where they have some openin's…" Grimacing at this twisted sense of humor, they stare at the man seated by the fireplace. Quaid shrugs and combs the stem of his pipe through his beard. "Poor taste, I s'pose…" He sets his pipe aside and picks up a metal can from a bin of food. "Hmm… Government peaches…"

One of the men laughs gruffly, spits aside on the floor, and tosses his drink back. "You talk but have nothin' to say." Extending his cup to be refilled, he tries to keep his hand from trembling. The others standing at the counter continue to stare as the frontiersman opens the canned fruit.

Eventually, Quaid continues. "Whatever it is out there that has crazed my woman, has us holed up in this place like a boxed meal ripe fer the harvest. If we start headin' out of here one by one, it'll pick us off." Turning the can as he opens it, Quaid looks at the line of men, everyone trying to veil their fear. "We need to stick together and come up with a plan of attack. That, or at least a good defense…"

VII

Near the abandoned logging camp, the aircraft sits at the edge of the tree line, half-buried in the snow. Despite the tilted angle of the airframe and a broken wing strut, the flying machine doesn't look terribly damaged. The bad weather has passed, and a steel grey sky looms over the freshly fallen snow.

The pilot unloads sacks of supplies from the aircraft, and the navigator sits on a snowbank, staring toward the camp. "This damn place gives me the creeps."

Wings tosses the last parcel out of the airplane and jumps down to the ground. "Me, too… But hey, that's why they're paying us double. Let's get to work. The S.P.E.C. crew

Flight of the Windigo

arrives in a few days, and we have a camp to set up."

"What if they don't show up?"

Wings pulls a small stogie from his coat and lights it. "They'll show. And, as soon as they arrive, we're outta here."

Placing his hand on the grip of his sidearm, Pooch pulls the gun from the holster and spins the cylinder to see that it is loaded all around. "If it comes for us, I'm gonna give it all six."

"Hmm… Do you think six will take care of of 'em all?"

Taken aback, the navigator nervously asks, "You think there's more?"

Wings takes a puff from the cigar and gazes toward the abandoned camp. "I've never seen or heard of anything like it." He shakes his head as he looks around. "But, to see bodies hung up like that, and some of 'em mutilated… What kind of man or beast could do that to all those folks?"

Pooch, still holding his pistol, trepidatiously looks to the nearby woods. "It still brings bile to my throat to think about it. I'm not looking forward to seeing that camp again, I tell ya."

Wings grabs his rifle and then goes to sling some sacks over his shoulder. Looking down the path to camp, he remarks, "Let's get set up before dark."

Pooch holsters his pistol and grabs a bundle of supplies. "As soon as S.P.E.C. gets here, we're gone?"

"Just as soon as they set foot in the camp…"

"The moment I lay eyes on them, I'll be in the airplane and warming the boiler!"

~*~

Walking into the logging camp, they automatically look to the treetops. The stark branches sway in the chilling breeze. They soon stand outside of one of the larger tents near the middle of the camp. As the afternoon sunlight begins to fade, Wings scans the forest canopy. "Notice anything different?"

"Yeah…"

They drop what they're carrying and stare upward. Pooch finally turns and gulps. "Where did the rest of them go?"

"I don't know."

Wings peels open the flap of the tent and peeks inside. "We'll set up in here for now." He tosses the supply sacks through the doorway and turns to walk back to the plane.

Pooch does the same with what he's carrying and calls out to Wings. "Where could they have gone?"

Flight of the Windigo

Reverently, Wings stops and speaks over his shoulder. "Whatever it was that put 'em up there could have come back." As Pooch follows Wings through the quiet camp, a sick feeling churns in his gut. He chokes down the bile rising from his stomach and peers back up to the treetops. "I can't wait to be rid of this place."

~*~

At the trading post, the men stand drinking at the bar. Several oil lanterns are lit to offset the fading daylight still shimmering through the windows. Intoxicated expressions hardly conceal the fright building behind their weary eyes. Outside, the Indian woman's wailing continues and then suddenly ceases. In the eerie silence, the men look at each other. One of the hunters steps to the middle of the room, perks his ears and mutters, "D'ya hear that?"

Seated by the fireplace, Quaid glances all around. "Yeah... Somethin's amiss..."

The only sound is from the occasional gust of wind that rattles the windowpanes. The hunter circles the stove and tilts his head to listen better. "Do you think she passed?"

One of the men suggests, "Maybe she's feeling better?"

Everyone turns to him with skeptical stares. The tavern owner uncorks another jug and refills drinks. He grumbles, "Who's going to muster up enough courage to go and check?"

Quaid swirls the contents of his tin cup and finishes it. "Well, I figure I'm the one responsible for 'er, so I should do it." He gets up, fastens his fur coat and walks over to the door. "Better to check in on 'er 'fore dark." With everyone watching, he stands hesitantly at the doorway.

With a thud, the proprietor slams his jug on the bar. "Holly damnation…! She bin out there more'n a day already… It can wait till mornin'."

Quaid lifts the metal latch and swings the door open, letting a cold blast of air in. When he steps outside one of the men goes over to close the door, swing the heavy latch back into place, and then backs away. As the incessant wind blows, everyone silently stares at the door.

Eventually, there is a pounding on the door. Guns held at the ready, the men watch, as one of them goes to open it. After the latch is unlocked, the door opens to let in another blast of frigid air. Quaid steps inside and slams the heavy wooden door closed behind him. He takes a deep breath, slides the locking bolt, and turns to face the room. In his mitts, he holds the heavy, linked chain that once held the captive.

Flight of the Windigo

Quaid steps past the men staring at him. He tosses the chains on the bar and goes back to his seat near the fireplace. Awestruck, they stare at the thick metal links. A lumberjack timidly inquires, "Them dogs get to 'er?"

Quaid slowly shakes his head and then takes his pipe out of his pocket. "She warn't near to them dogs."

A hunter lifts one of the broken links and inspects it. "That's impossible... Them chains were secure."

Stepping over to take a closer look, the tavern owner studies the bindings and then glances at the man with the bandage over his nose. "No wonder she bit through your nose like it was soft cheese." He holds up the empty restraints to show that they had been gnawed through. Over in the corner, the glow of a flame flickers on Quaid's features, as he lights his clay pipe.

VIII

The caravan of wagons halts before several downed trees blocking the path. To check on the situation, Hammer and Evans proceed through the snow to the head of the convoy. Hammer kicks his boot to one of the fallen timbers and grunts, "Dis is da turd stand of trees dat has fallen in our path."

Evans grins. "*Turd?*"

Hammer brushes snow from his pant leg and looks at her strangely. "Ya, *turd*... Where you been?"

Flight of the Windigo

Eyes twinkling, Evans scans the woods for any sign of natural distress. "Yeah… It's starting to look suspicious."

When Hammer gives the nod, a clearing crew starts in with axes to hack away at the obstacles. Watching them work, he hollers, "Cut 'er wide, so's da wagon hubs kin clear by at least a foot!" Unfolding a map, Evans looks over to her partner and waves him closer. Leaning in, Hammer scratches his beard and asks, "What's our arrival lookin' ta be?"

Evans makes an estimation of their location and then marks it in relation to the other blockades. "Between cutting through trees and diverting around obstructions, this has cost us three days so far…. Plotting each of the blocked locations on the map shows our winding path thus far… It's as if we're being directed on a predetermined course…"

"Ya mean, we're bein' toyed wit?"

"Appears that way…"

They watch the crew chop at the pile of uprooted trees. Confounded, Hammer tilts his head. "Dem trees are pulled up, not felled… *How can dat be?*"

She looks at the markings on the map and offers a shrug. "All I can do is interpret what the map is telling me."

Puffing up to his full height, his hands on his hips, Hammer sticks his chest out and bellows, "Well, I say bring 'em on, den! If a few loose-rooted trees is all dey can throw at us, den we'll have easy work of 'em when da steam mill is set up." Lifting his arm up with a finger outstretched, the big man points forward. "Onward, men!!!"

Over her spectacles, Evans peers at Hammer and gives an amused chuckle. The sound of impatient draft animals in creaking wagon rigging and the steady thwack of chopping axes echoes through the forest.

~*~

In a tent at the center of camp, Wings takes inventory, sorting through a stack of provisions. He startles when he hears footsteps approaching from outside and reaches for his rifle. "Pooch…?" As the tent flap rustles, Wings cocks back the hammer of his gun, but he relaxes when his navigator steps in. Then, he notices the object held in Pooch's hand. "What's that?"

Pooch puts a loosely wrapped bundle of cloth on a table. It falls partly open to reveal sharp pieces of shattered bone. Feeling ill, the copilot makes a grim face and morbidly states, "It's something I found…" He shivers, gestures outside and then looks back at the object on the table. "This particular one is a forearm with a hand. The flesh is nearly picked clean."

"Human?"

"Still had some shirt sleeve on it…"

Wings stares at the gruesome item a moment before looking back to Pooch. "Was there more?"

"Stuff like that is *all over* the place. Tucked in corners, behind boxes, under beds…" The unnerved navigator plops himself in a chair. "It's like dozens of cannibals were out here having a feast. Most of it's frozen… *Some* of it still seems *fresh!*"

"*Fresh?!?*"

"Yeah, *recent.* Like it happened since we were last here. I found a piece with muscle that was still soft."

Wings stares at the severed limb. Reaching down, he gingerly peels back the cloth. He examines the chew marks on the exposed bone and then asks, "What's *your* take on all this?"

"Something evil has come to this place…"

Wings swallows hard, nods, and covers the arm back up. "No more exploring camp… We're not paid to be undertakers. We hold up here until the S.P.E.C. crew arrives. We sign this operation off to them, and then we head out directly."

Spooked by a sudden gust of wind, the navigator glances at the door flap and then looks over to his partner. "They were supposed to be here a *week* ago."

"Probably the bad weather… They'll be here soon."

"I think we should think about lighting-out right now. Things ain't right, and I have a bad feeling about this place."

"The *safest* place for now is to hole up *right here.*"

Unsure, Pooch shakes his head. "We could take our gear and make a camp by the aircraft."

"With the unusually severe winds we've been having, we'd be too exposed to the elements out there. Here, at least we have this shelter to protect us."

Pooch is silent for a moment, then nods his agreement. "Alright, partner… But, I don't like it. I think the longer we stick around, the worse off we'll be."

The pilot glances at the table and then over to his copilot. "We'll keep together at all times. We'll watch out for each other… Don't even squat in the woods to do your business without me there to guard your backside."

Cracking a smile, Pooch chuckles, relieving the tension. "We've been together a long-time, partner. I hate the thought of us going out as part of a human buffet."

"If things get any more peculiar, we'll pull up stakes and fly out without looking back."

"How could things get any *more* peculiar?"

"Let's just give it a few more days."

"Okay, Wings..."

The pilot looks to the tent flap as it flutters in the wind. "The S.P.E.C. crew will soon be here."

Pooch tosses the limb outside. "I'm with you, pard."

IX

The wind whips against the walls of the outpost. At the bar, several rugged frontiersmen load guns and layer on more clothes before venturing outdoors. The relentless winter storm continues, and they are visibly frightened, in spite of the exaggerated show of weaponry.

Nearby, smoking his pipe, Quaid sits observing them. He glances over to Fenimore, standing vigilant at the window, then back to the group of hunters. With a cough, he clears his throat and speaks to one of the woodsmen who looks his way. "D'ya really think you'll find 'er?"

"We'll find her, alright. Ain't an animal we can't track. We'll bring her back or put her down."

Quaid lowers his pipe stem. "She's been a good woman, till the other day… I'd ruther you bring her back.

Fenimore turns his attention to their conversation. "No, she is *Windigo*… You should not try to bring her back."

The hunter looks to Fenimore, pats his rifle and declares, "Windigo or not, we'll take care of it. Any other requests?"

Fenimore pivots away from the window and cautiously puts his back to the wall, as if something from the forest was suddenly watching him. His bearded features void of emotion, he replies, "To stop it, you must cut out its heart and burn it. The *Windigo* heart is ice, and you must melt it to stop the evil."

Skeptical, the armed men look at each other. One of them dismissively spits and shakes his head. "Are you coming with us to kill this thing or not?"

As if in a trance, Fenimore responds in a vacant tone. "No… I will not chance to cross the path of a *Windigo*."

The hunter cradles his rifle over his arm and grunts, "Whole lot'a help you are. Tell ya what… Jest stick right here, stay warm, and tell yer ghost stories. I'll bring the thing's heart, and ya can cook it any way ya'd like."

With weapons cocking and feet stomping, the hunting party heads to the door and files outside. As the blustery weather sweeps in, Quaid tucks his pipe close to his chest to keep the glow in the bowl from dying. After the door shuts, he considers the remaining lumberjacks standing at the bar and then turns to see the trapper peering out the window again. "Fenimore, you bin livin' up here yer whole life. Ya gonna let 'em wander around lookin' for a Windigo in this weather? What're you *really* afraid of…?"

Keeping still, Fenimore watches the men pass by the window, trudge through the storm and disappear into the forest. With dark, glazed over eyes, he turns to stare at Quaid. "I am not afraid of any mortal being. What I fear is the creature who turned your woman into a *Windigo*."

"We ne'er saw any sort of creature."

"*She* did…"

Staring back at Fenimore, Quaid lets out a puff of smoke from his pipe.

~*~

Flight of the Windigo

Seated at a long, wooden table in the largest of the tents, Wings and Pooch play a hand of cards. The light fades as dusk approaches, and an intermittent wind flutters the unsecured door flap. Wings puts his cards face-down and strikes a match to light an oil lamp. He looks at Pooch and then tilts his head toward the doorway. "Last call for the privy…"

Standing, Pooch lays his cards on the table. "I gotta go."

Pushing back his chair, Wings grabs his rifle and then picks up the glowing lamp. "Alright… Let's go."

A few yards from their headquarters, they circle around a canvassed A-frame that is set off separate from the other tents. Wings tosses the door flap aside, shines the lamp and peeks in. "All clear." In the dim light, Pooch scans the woods one more time before ducking into the latrine tent.

Standing guard outside, Wings shivers in his leather overcoat as a strong blast of wind passes by. The lamp flickers, nearly blowing out, and the pilot shifts his position to shield the flame with his body. Suddenly, a gunshot rips through the tent wall, followed by a fearful scream.

Dropping the lamp, Wings spins and shoulders his rifle. "*Pooch…?!?*" The lamp glass breaks when it hits the ground. Oil spills out, catches fire and then flares into a ball of flames. The terrifying screams continue and another shot tears through the canvas. Rifle ready, Wings jerks the tent's flap door open.

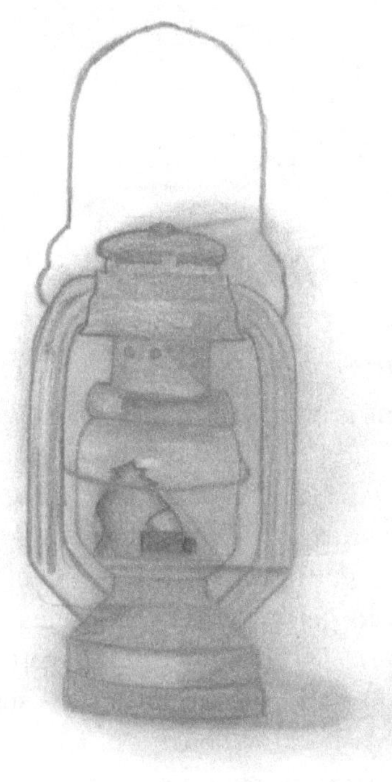

X

The barrel of his pistol still smoking, Pooch lies on the ground. The spirit-possessed Indian woman hunches over top of him, as flames lick the canvas wall. Gnashing her razor-sharp teeth, she turns to Wings at the doorway and lets out a guttural growl. Desperately, Pooch squirms to get away. He screeches, *"Get her away from me!!!!"* Repeatedly, the woman snaps her jaw like an iron spring trap, as she lunges at Pooch's neck. When he blocks her attack with his arm, she chomps down on it with the force of a rabid dog. Wailing, Pooch tries to twist free. *"Shoot her…!!!"*

A bullet from the rifle tumbles the crazed woman to the side of the tent, and Wings quickly chambers another round, ready to shoot again. He rushes to his friend and notices the torn coat sleeve. Eyes wide, Pooch squirms away from her, pointing as she scrambles out under the canvas wall. "I'm fine! Go *get* her…!!" Leading with his rifle, Wings dashes outside.

Not far from the burning tent, Wings scans the woods. There is a smear of fresh blood where the woman slipped out of the tent, but no other sign of her trail. Pooch, clutching his injured arm, arrives holding his pistol. Wings turns to him. "Wasn't that the woman who was with that Quaid fella?"

"She did look kinda familiar, *before* she flipped out."

Behind them, the tent canvas continues to brightly burn, and they warily search the trees to the far reaches of the light. Wings keeps his rifle tucked to his shoulder ready to shoot. "What *happened* in there?"

"Don't know… A gust of wind blew through the flap, and suddenly she was there."

"Are you okay…?"

In the firelight, Pooch peels back the ripped sleeve and uncovers the wound on his arm. "She's got teeth like knives. Cut through two shirts *and* my long-handle underwear."

As he inspects the bleeding bite marks, Wings grimaces. "We better get that cleaned up." Backing their way to the camp, Wings and Pooch keep their guns pointed toward the darkness. Slowly, they retreat through the fading light of the burning latrine to their headquarters in the big tent.

~*~

The hunting party trudges through the frozen, frontier landscape. Due to their evident lack of progress, faces are grim. One of the hunters raises a hand to halt the others. "Let's hold up here a while..." With rifles tucked loosely under their arms, the men look around while warming their hands by blowing into their gloves. The leader points ahead, across a stretch of frozen lake, to what appears to be an opening in the forest. "That clearing in the trees looks familiar."

The man directly behind him moves forward and nods. "We was very near to here jest yesterday."

"If so, where are our tracks?"

"They ain't here now, but I'm sure we were here."

After the group searches for any sign of them being there the day prior, they turn to their leader for answers. One of them speaks up. "There's no trail hereabout. How much further will we drift with nothing to track?"

As they look out over the familiar countryside, another man mutters, "I swear, we were here jest yesterday…"

Looking behind to the path they just created and then to the untrod territory ahead, leads to a questioning grumble amongst the group and then a universal nod of agreement. The man in the lead states, "We'll travel across the lake to that stand of trees to verify our trail and then return to the trading post." Their weapons held at the ready, the hunting party keeps close, as they wade into the deep snow.

~*~

The northern winds blow in forceful gusts that rattle icicles clinging to the tips of frozen tree branches. High above, storm clouds roll with thunder, moving swiftly across the darkening sky. The ominous weather sweeps across the open terrain, as the hunters wade through waist-high drifts of snow. Mysteriously, the storm circles around to their flank and then hovers at the edge of the trees.

The leader suddenly stops in the middle of the clearing and stares down at the snow before him. As the others slowly gather alongside, one of them asks, "What is it…?"

The man stands looking down at tracks, perpendicular to their own, cut through the snow. "Looks to be a trail of sorts."

"Ours…?"

"No…"

"From the woman?

"I don't *think* so…"

A man crosses the strange trail to inspect it. "It looks to be somethin' else…"

Apprehensively, the group puts their backs together, forming a circle, with each man looking out to the nearby tree line or across the barren lakescape. One of the men peers back over his shoulder to the unusual trail and asks, "If not ours, who's is it? What kind of thing could cut that swath…?"

Another man steps across the cut trail and travels parallel to its sunken path, trying to identify any familiar sign. "It might've been her if she was pullin' a sled, maybe…" Directly above, the storm swirls around and starts to close in. The man studying the track feels a forceful shiver of electricity travel through his entire body. Unexpectedly, he throws off his mitts as if they are on fire. Feeling something completely foreign within, he looks at his exposed hands and then at the men around him, staring.

Flight of the Windigo

One of them asks, "What's *wrong* with you?"

He looks up to the stormy skies and blinks several times to see more clearly. "Something isn't right here..."

Then, the man who first crossed the odd trail discharges a firearm, and one of the others is blown back into a snowbank. A silent moment of shock is broken, when another deafening gunshot sprays blood across the snow. Low, rumbling clouds churn overhead, as gunshots blast from each man standing in the clustered circle. The intense exchange of gunfire abruptly ends with the entire group laid out in a ring of corpses.

XI

Wings and Pooch stand beside their airplane examining the steam engine and an obvious crack in the boiler. Disheartened, Wings shakes his head and looks to his copilot. "Didn't you drain the water, like I asked?"

"Yes. I checked it twice." Wings puts a gloved finger to the crack, knocks away the scab of ice and a trickle of water leaks out. Embarrassed that he apparently missed something, Pooch mutters, "I swear... I drained it *all*." He looks at the pilot. "Is that it for us?"

"That's it for the boiler."

The navigator looks over his shoulder back to the camp. "Then..., we're *stuck* here?"

Flight of the Windigo

"We can either wait for the S.P.E.C. crew that's a week late, or we can walk out of here with whatever we can carry."

"Walk to where?"

Wings leans on the aircraft and gazes into the distance. "Pull out that map of yours, and let's take a look." Pooch digs through his shoulder bag and pulls out a chart. He unfolds the map, and Wings studies the topography. "That fellow, Quaid, said there was a trading post a few days walk south of here. Wasn't that where he was headed?"

Pooch glances at his bandaged arm. "Who knows if he even *made* it there, what with that crazed woman?"

They study the map to get their bearings. Wings points to an area directly south of their location. "Near that lake, there's a spot along the river that would make a good place for a trading post. I'm willing to bet it's there."

Pooch stares at the wide expanse of territory and then looks at Wings. "Are you kidding?"

"No. I think we should head that way."

"There could be nothing there."

"That river is the best place to set up for trade."

"It's a long shot, at best…"

"Maybe… Any other ideas?"

The navigator considers their options. "If we make a heading to the southeast, we might run into the S.P.E.C. crew or maybe cross their trail."

"Then, what? Come back here…?"

Heaving a sigh, the navigator looks at the map again. "They'll *never* believe what we've seen."

"Yeah… They'll be low on supplies and probably send us off to find the trading post, which is what we're being paid to do in the first place."

Nodding his head in agreement, Pooch looks back at their location on the map and traces his finger along the path the logging crew should be following. "They must be close…"

"We've been saying that for days now." Wings stares at the map. "I'd say the post is about two-day's walk from here. We can carry enough food to keep us until we find it and be back here in less than a week. The replacement crew should be here by then, and we can use their equipment to fix our boiler."

Wincing in pain, Pooch cradles his wound and nods. "Alright, let's try it. *Anything* beats waiting around here."

~*~

Flight of the Windigo

Making their way, the S.P.E.C. wagons are once again held up by a jam of fallen trees. Hammer stands on the back of a wagon looking around, searching the woodland. To the north, he sees an opening in the forest, and he yells ahead to the cutting crew. "Leave it be dis time… We'll be goin' 'round…" He points to a wide spot where they can get through the trees. With a series of commands followed by whip cracks and the creaking of wagon wheels, the party turns off-trail and proceeds toward the snowy clearing that can be seen beyond.

The teams pull the heavy loads through the deep snow, each wagon having an easier time than the one preceding it. Evans snowshoes her way to Hammer, eventually catching him when the wagons stop at the clearing. Hammer stands with his clenched fists perched on his hips, looking out over an expanse of treeless terrain. As she comes up next to him, he turns to her. "What d'ya tink 'bout dat?"

"Looks to be a snow-covered lake."

Hammer stomps the ground with his boot and grunts. "Da question is, how stable is it?" Motioning for several crewmen with picks and shovels to move forward, he hollers, "Head out dere, and see how tick dat ice is under all dat snow." He looks at Evans, as she wipes the fog from her glasses. "Where are we on dat map of yourn?"

Evans takes a folded map from her pocket and spreads it out on the side of a wagon. She points to their destination. "The camp should be not too far on the other side of the lake."

"So, dis could be a shorter route?"

"Possibly..."

They watch as the workers clear a patch of snow and start picking at the frozen surface. Hammer shrugs, satisfied. "Seems ta be hard 'nough..."

As she takes a closer look at their position on the map, Evans shakes her head. "I don't like it. We're already days late."

"More reason ta move straight across..."

She looks at him and then back to the men chipping ice. "If we have to lose a wagon, which one would you choose?"

Hammer thinks for a moment before responding. "Yaugh, point taken..." As chips of ice fly into the air with each strike of a pickaxe, Hammer peers over his shoulder back to the path they made through the woods. "We'll have to turn dem back to da trail, den?"

Evans shakes her head. "That trail has slowed us down." Putting her finger to the map, she traces a route around the perimeter of the lake. "If we follow the edges, we can stay on the ice and be close enough to pull out if we get into trouble."

Hammer shrugs. "Da shoreline is never da fastest way."

"In this case, it *might* be. We won't have to clear anymore fallen trees, and we can cut across some of the smaller inlets."

Nearby, the crew breaks through the ice, and they measure its thickness with an axe handle. Hammer gives them a whirl of his hand, signaling them to return to their wagons. Folding her map and returning it to her pocket, Evans watches Hammer plod through the snow to confer with the crew. Pointing back at her, he then waves his arm toward the shore and plods onward.

Menacing storm clouds linger over the frozen landscape, as the wagons, keeping to the shore, get on their way. A chilling gust of wind sweeps across the snow-covered lake and blows past them toward the tree-lined shore.

XII

Those that remain at the outpost gather at the fireplace to watch Fenimore, wearing a set of goggles with dark lenses, poke the glowing coals with metalworking tools. From the fire, he pulls a forged piece of metal that has eye slits and a beak-shaped nose with breathing holes. He bends the sides of the red-hot piece to finish the shape of the mask.

A curious logger asks, "Are you making that ugly thing to scare away ghosts?"

With a puff of pipe smoke, Quaid remarks, "Fenimore, ya think that's gonna protect ya from it?"

Flight of the Windigo

The glass of Fenimore's goggles reflect the fire's flames. He turns to them and then, specifically, turns to the man that is missing a nose. He quenches the metal facemask in a bucket of water and then examines it. "The Windigo has begun the season of feeding... Its appetite will only get more ravenous." He turns the mask over and holds it close to his face, looking out through the eye slits. Then, he sticks it back into the coals. "It feeds on the tastiest of morsels. The nose, lips, and eyes..." The trapper's crude metalwork, accompanied by his deliberate words, sends shivers up the spines of those men observing. Some, morbidly thinking about losing those tasty parts, involuntarily touch their faces.

Eventually, the men move across the room to take stock of provisions. Gradually, the inside of the station turns into a survival workshop, as each man gathers and assembles any type of protective gear possible.

~*~

The airmen, laden with supply packs, trudge through freshly fallen snow. Pooch grips his injured arm and shivers. He is beginning to feel very ill, and his features have darkened. As they march through the maze of trees, his arm gets more painful. Wings stops to take out the map and, concerned, glances over at his partner. "How're you feelin', Pooch?"

The navigator tries to straighten his arm and winces. "None too good… I don't think I could even hold up that map, let alone read it, what with my vision blurring as much as it is. My whole body is starting to ache and stove up."

Wings glances down at the map and then looks out to the seemingly endless expanse of wilderness. "I don't think we should make camp for the night without some shelter in case another storm blows in."

The sick copilot nods in agreement. "I'll keep moving as long as I can."

"Want me to look at that arm again?"

Stopping to lean against a tree, Pooch shakes his head. "No… I think we've done all that can be done for it."

Wings eyes his friend. "You let me know if we need to take a break and swap those bandages out for fresh ones."

Pooch puts on his bravest face and cradles the wounded limb close to his chest. "Thanks, pard." Wings folds the map, tucks it away, and glances one more time at his sick companion before continuing on through the deep snow.

~*~

Flight of the Windigo

A cold, winter night sets on the caravan. At the edge of the forest, along the frozen shoreline, several cookfires are lit. Seated in a camp chair near one of the wagons, Evans studies her map and considers their slow progress. Hammer walks over and pulls up his own chair to sit with her. In silence, he looks out over the blanket of snow covering the lake. At length, he mutters, "Dis endeavor has not started off too well…"

She glances over at him. "No… It has not."

Still staring at the silvery, moonlit snow, he continues. "We're goin' ta be short of a lot of men when we have ta send for more supplies. Wit da trails being what dey are, we will need dem to clear as dey go."

"It's not marked on this map, but I have information that there could be an independently operated trading post a few days south of the logging site, near where the river widens. Looks like we bypassed the turn-off because of the blockages. It's located on the main waterway and could be the best route, come spring."

"Spring is a long way off."

"The pilots who scouted the location were scheduled to bring in supplies. We should be set for a while. I figure we can get other things in and out through them, if need be."

The gruff machinist scratches some clinging ice from his beard and turns to Evans. "Hell, I don't trust dem airheads. Most likely, dey dropped all our supplies from da sky, skedaddled out of dere as fast as dey could, 'n left it for da woodsy critters ta pick tru. We were to be dere days ago, and I doubt dat dey stuck 'round."

Pulling her fur-lined collar up, Evans shivers and sets the map aside. "We'll see. Not sure what to expect when we get to this camp… Who knows what remained when they left?"

"Dey most likely didn't leave any decent sort of vittles, or dey wouldn't have took off."

Evans adjusts her glasses and nods. "Once we're there, we'll find out. Should make it by the evening of the morrow…"

Hammer grunts and digs his heel into the snowpack. "More'n a week behind on da schedule already…"

~*~

In the dark, winter sky, looming storm clouds circle, blocking out the stars, patrolling across the wilderness. After hovering above the lake, the peculiar weather gradually travels on toward the trading post. The cold winds rake through the treetops, searching.

XIII

Wings wakes with a shiver. Sheltered under broken tree limbs and covered with a dusting of morning snow, he sits up to look at his partner. Sweeping the powdery snow from Pooch's body, he stares in shock at the navigator's zombie-like appearance. The injured man's features are that of a corpse. Hollow-eyed, with skin turned dark grey… His lips are shriveled, bloodless and cracked. "Pooch…?" Wings startles, when the navigator's eyes abruptly shoot open. "Partner, you look like hell…"

"Wings… I feel worse."

"Do you think you can get up?"

"I can hardly move at all, and my chest feels so cold."

Wings shakes out a blanket and wraps it around his friend. "Hang tight. I'll try to carry you the rest of the way."

"No… Just leave me. I don't feel right."

While gathering gear, Wings glances back to his copilot. "Don't say that. You're coming with me. We'll get you some warm food and a fire, and you'll be feeling better in no time."

As Pooch convulses into shivering, he attempts to put on a smile in spite of the situation. "Sure thing… I'll be fine."

~*~

The sky over the trading post is dark and ominous. Quaid stands at the doorway staring outside. He watches Fenimore move to the corner of the building to scan the woods. Quaid's warm breath lingers in a fog, as it hits the frigid air. "Them hunters ain't comin' back alive, are they?"

Fenimore looks back and shakes his head.

"Any chance of *us* makin' it out of these woods?"

Taking his time, Fenimore finally nods and then replies. "The heart of the Windigo is as cold as ice. It feasts on those who enter its winter realm. We must burn out the infestation at the logging camp to kill it."

Pulling up the collar of his bearskin coat, Quaid winces. "Don't 'specially like the notion of goin' back there again. Figured this world was big 'nough ta n'er cross *that* trail twice." His breath forms tiny icicles on his moustache, as he strokes his beard whiskers. "Ya figur' my woman is back there?"

The trapper tilts his head upward to the cold, grey sky. "If she is Windigo, she is there…"

Quaid reaches a hand inside his coat to scratch his chest. With a grunt, he mutters, "With all this damned cold weather, sure wouldn't mind havin' her body to warm my bed again." Questioning Quaid's motives, Fenimore drops his gaze from the sky to give him a judgmental look.

"Maybe you should get a dog…"

When an odd sound from the woods catches their attention, they lift their rifles. Soon, in the distance, a large figure can faintly be seen approaching through the trees. Fenimore puts on his protective goggles. Then, he raises the metal mask to his face and fastens it on. Rifle aimed into the woods, Quaid peers at the trapper over the receiver of his gun. "Fenimore, you got 'nother of them mask 'n goggles for *me?*" With a shake of his head, Fenimore sights his own weapon.

Stumbling from the woods, Wings comes into view, carrying supply packs and cradling his friend in his arms. Spotting the two men outside the trading post, he calls out. "Hello...! Lend me a hand!!"

Quaid glances over to the trapper and cocks the hammer on his rifle. "Fenimore... Is he Windigo?"

After a prolonged pause, while the burdened figure stumbles closer, Fenimore lowers his rifle, removes his facemask and shakes his head. "No... He is not Windigo. *Yet...*"

~*~

The men crowd near the fireplace, as Wings tends to his friend's wound. Wood is added to the fire, and the blaze lights up the room. One man moves closer and, over the pilot's shoulder, asks, "What happened to him?"

Finished with changing bandages and re-wrapping the wound, Wings shakes out a blanket and tucks it around his sick friend. He turns to face the group of wary onlookers and responds. "We were setting up supplies for the replacement crew at the Kishwaukee Valley Lumber Mill camp."

Flight of the Windigo

Standing at the back of the group, Quaid, interested, smokes his pipe and listens. A man asks, "*What logging camp…?* Do you mean the *massacred camp?*"

Another man pipes in. "Who would want to work that site after everyone was *killed?!?*"

Sensing that the situation could get hostile, Wings surveys the anxious crowd. He is about to reply, when Quaid steps in and grumbles at them, "Quiet now, ya chicken-livers… Let the man say his piece." He checks the condition of Pooch, and then faces Wings. "What happened to 'im?"

Glancing around at the troubled faces in the room, Wings explains. "He was attacked by a crazed Indian woman." His stare stops on Quaid.

"Was it my squaw perhaps?"

The aviator scans the attentive faces again and nods. "Yeah, I think it was. At least it could've been…" The room instantly buzzes with talk of the woman, her grim condition, and what might have happened to those who went after her. The word *Windigo* gradually enters the heated exchange. Mention of the injured navigator and what he might become also enters the passionate discussion.

Quaid takes a step toward Fenimore and whispers, "Outside, you jest said to me that he *warn't* no Windigo…"

Prudently, the trapper lowers his goggles over his eyes and takes the metal mask from his pouch. The discussion in the room intensifies, and the focus turns to the necessary precautions that should be taken. Sensing the quickly developing ill-will directed toward them, Wings slightly turns away and eases his pistol from its holster. He warily eyes his rifle leaning against the wall. Someone in the crowd declares, "He must be Windigo! If he's bin attacked by that crazy gal, he's *infected!*"

Quaid looks at the men who had been bitten previously. "What 'bout you two…? You ain't turned Windigo."

"We ain't sick lookin'."

Someone retorts, "But, ya ain't any easier to look at!"

Another adds, "We have to cut out his heart and *burn* it!"

From the back of the room a man replies, "The best thing to do is put him down, before he can harm anyone else…"

The man with the bandage in place of a nose exclaims, "Let's do it before it's too late!!!"

With his pistol in hand, Wings pivots to face the room. He fans the gun barrel at the surrounding men. In a measured tone, he speaks slowly and deliberately. "*No one* comes near him…"

XIV

"Windigo killed the men at that camp! If he's been attacked, he's one, too!" In response to the comment, the men advance. Wings backs up to the bed and positioning to defend his friend. As he methodically points his pistol at each man approaching, he declares, "We saw for ourselves what had happened there. This man had *no part* in it. He's *hurt* and won't harm *anyone!*" The hostile crowd mills nervously and some of them begin to brandish their weapons.

A man calls out from the back of the group. "*Windigo!* We hav'ta cut out his *heart* and *burn* 'im!"

Flight of the Windigo

Before anyone can rush in, Wings shoots his pistol, knocking the kettle from the cook stove. Using the distraction, he quickly flips his gun to his left hand. He snatches his rifle from near the bedside and cocks the firearm, ready for what comes next. The crowd pauses to reassess the situation. Someone murmurs, "He's only one, and we're many…"

Aiming his rifle from the hip, Wings fires at one of the whiskey bottles on the bar, shattering it. One-handed, he spin-cocks the lever action rifle, as he hollers, "You *want* to die?!? *Come on ahead…!!!*"

"But… He's *Windigo…!!!*"

Wings turns the aim of his pistol to the speaker and replies in a commanding voice. "If he is harmed, there will be others who will be feeling the hurt soon after!" The aviator lowers the barrel of the rifle across the arm holding his pistol, and fans the crowd with both weapons. When his aim lingers on one of the loggers, the man meekly utters, "We saw what happened to that woman… If *he* turns, how will you protect us from *him?*"

Standing firm, Wings addresses everyone in the room. "You have my word on it. I'll stay at his side. If he turns bad, *I'll* be the one to put him down."

From the back of the room, Fenimore speaks out. "Wait. He may not be *full* Windigo..." As they step aside, the trapper, wearing his goggles and metal mask, comes forward.

Someone mutters, "Let Fenimore take a look at 'im."

Another man grumbles. "Yer endangerin' *all* of us."

Holding his ground, Wings turns the aim of his weapons toward Fenimore. "Who are you to decide anything?"

Removing his mask, he speaks calmly. "I am Fenimore. I have lived amongst the Ojibway for nigh on four lustrums. From them, I learned the legend of the Windigo, and I *know* the signs of its deadly evil."

Considering the expertise of the trapper, Wings glances over his shoulder at his sick partner and then nods his consent. "Alright... Come on forward and have a look... Drop that blade to show your good will."

When the knife is drawn from its sheath and dropped, the pointed tip sticks the large blade upright in the plank floor. While his guns keep the others at bay, Wings lets Fenimore step forward to examine his friend. The trapper puts his protective mask back on and cautiously leans over the deathly-ill copilot. He

Flight of the Windigo

pulls back the blanket to study him, letting his gaze linger on the bandaged arm.

Pooch opens his eyes and is startled when he sees the figure in the metal mask. They stare curiously at one another, until Fenimore mutters through the protective face shield. "*Windigo*... Is that *you* inside this man?"

Quaid taps the ash of his pipe out on his palm and asks, "*So...?* Is he Windigo or not?

Fenimore turns to look intently at the surrounding men. Then, he removes his mask and lifts the goggles from his eyes. "No..." Shaking his head, he adds, "He is very sick. He *will* die, but he is not Windigo. *Yet...*"

Moving back to position himself between Fenimore and his sick friend, Wings inquires, "What do you mean, *yet?*"

"The spirit of Windigo can suddenly arise in any of us. The evil of the north preys on wounded, weak, and hungry." As the trapper speaks, everyone creeps closer, curious to get a better look at Pooch. Wings pushes them back, but not as forcefully as before. He speaks to both Fenimore and the crowd. "He'll get better with some food in him."

The trapper returns his gaze to the sick man on the bed. "Sometimes Windigo can mislead. If he gets well, slow is better. *Too* fast... It is possible that an evil spirit has taken control."

"Don't you worry none. I'll watch over him."

A lumberjack asks, "What about them others who went huntin' after that crazy woman of his?" He looks to Quaid. "And, whoever butchered that logging camp...?" Pipe stem clenched in his teeth, a trickle of smoke seeps from Quaid's mouth, as he matches the man's gaze.

Wings keeps everyone backed away. "We never crossed anyone's path coming from the camp, and she was there last. She disappeared into the trees, after I put a bullet in her."

A murmur of discontent fills the room again, and someone exclaims, "She's *Windigo!* We need to put her *down!*"

Wings lowers his guns and raises his voice. "A relief crew is due at the camp any time now! When he was attacked, they were already a week late."

A logger spits aside. "Those men need to be warned."

Quaid lets another puff of smoke escape from his lips. "Before more'n half of ya headed out to hunt down my woman, we planned to travel to that camp and burn all signs of evil."

Wings turns to Quaid. "That would be a hell of a blaze. Since we were there with you, the bodies in the trees have all disappeared, and the ones we buried have been dug up."

"Dug up?"

"We found bits and pieces stashed around the camp."

Quaid bites hard on his pipe. "All the more reason to burn the place and ever'thin' 'sociated with it."

Not keen on the idea of destroying everything, Wings shakes his head. "Our aircraft, with a busted boiler, is just outside the camp. We'd appreciate it if you didn't burn it too."

"Is that somethin' that can be fixed?"

The pilot nods. "As soon as my copilot's feeling better, we'll head back and get one of the steam engineers to repair it."

Peering down at the sick man shivering on the bed, Quaid shakes his head grimly. "He's lookin' none too good. And, there's no guarantee on them not destroyin' yer aircraft."

"I'll hold *you* accountable."

Taking the pipe from his mouth, Quaid blows smoke, leans in and speaks in a harsh whisper. "*Yeah...?* And, I'll hold *you* accountable for bringin' *that* sick man into *this* damn place. These brawny axe-heads are on edge and already 'bout to kill one another outta blind fear. On accounta some local folklore 'bout *flesh-eatin' spirits…*" The frontiersman's squinting eyes blaze with intensity. "You bringin' him here only reinforces the nightmares of these half-brained woodchoppers." He turns to look at them, as they slowly disperse to gather their gear. Then, after quickly glancing back at Pooch, he considers Wing's guns. "If ya plan to keep 'im alive, you'd better be ready to use those. Fear and hunger has a queer effect on the weak-minded…" Quaid gives the aviator a stern nod and retreats back to his seat by the fireplace. Returning to his pipe, he watches and waits for what will come next.

XV

Arriving at the logging camp, the S.P.E.C. crew begins to unload the wagons and settle in. With no sign of the recent massacre, the crew, expecting to resume the milling operation, diligently sets up their equipment.

At the big table in the headquarters tent, Evans works with calculation tools and a set of charts spread out before her. The canvas door-flap swings open wide and Hammer struts in. He notices the clutter on the table and grins. "Ev'rytin' is unloaded and bein' set up. We should have da crews cuttin' timber by da morrow."

Looking up from her work, Evans nods. "That's good."

Flight of the Windigo

"Won't take long ta set dis camp, since ev'ryting is still here from when da last crew left. Jest a bit of tidyin' up is all." From a crate, Hammer grabs a liquor bottle and two cups. Opposite Evans, he pulls a chair back from the table and pours them each a drink. "What was it dat happened to da last crew?"

She watches him, as he reaches over to set the drink on the blueprint in front of her. "They disappeared."

Hammer looks at his own drink and scratches his chin. "Why would dat be? Da lumber resources 'round here are some of da best I've seen."

"The ones in charge didn't say. In fact, they avoided it. And, when I inquired more, they acted awfully funny..."

Hammer lifts his cup, reaches across the table to clink it with hers and takes a drink. "Dem suits are always awful funny about givin' up da facts."

"Well, the more I questioned them about it, the more uncomfortable they became. And, the better the compensation to get us to come up here..." She lifts her cup and takes a sip.

"Dats peculiar..."

She peers up at him. "Huh?"

Hammer finishes his drink, pours another, and offers the opened bottle to Evans, who declines. "Dem aviators left a bunch of gear, but not much for food."

"You had it right, when you said not to rely on them."

"Funny ting is… A steam-powered flying machine is in da clearing jest outside da camp. Got a busted boiler…"

"Is it something you could fix?"

"Yep. Easy…"

She takes another sip from her drink and sets it aside. "Think they walked out?"

"Cain't figure why dey would light out… It's downright peaceful here. Da heavy winter ain't set in yet. We were only a week late, and dey should have brought 'nough food stores to last more'n a month."

Evans glances at a map on the table and then picks up a chart of the local topography. "I don't know where they might've gone… Let's get the timber harvest started tomorrow, while keeping a crew on the assembly of the mill." She leans on the table studying the lay of the land. After taking another gulp, Hammer peers at the map, as well. Evans points to an area close to the river, near a lake. "We're going to have to assign some men and wagons to venture to the trading post, if there is one." The engineer traces the route from their position on the map. "They can gather what might be available there and put an order in for more supplies. Maybe our pilots are there and can be brought back." As Hammer pours himself another refill, Evans continues. "If so, we can fix the airplane's boiler and get them on their way with a wish-list for our next delivery."

After finishing his last pour, Hammer sets his cup down and blows out a breath through rumbling lips. "Sounds good... Dis should be like a walk in da woods."

~*~

Firelight flickers on the men slumbering inside the trading post. The sounds of uneasy shifting of positions mixes with loud breathing and the occasional grunting snore. Outside, the incessant wind howls with forceful gusts that blast against the wood-framed structure.

Waking with a start, Wings eyes pop open. Fully alert, with guns at the ready, he sits up and scans the dimly lit room. Listening intently, he hears something of a groan. He turns to see Pooch lying in a mummy-like pose on the bunk behind him. A strong blast of wind rattles the fastened window shutters, and then all falls still. With his weapons held close, he lies back again. Relieved, Wings pulls his blanket up over his shoulders. Only the sounds of snoring and the popping crackle of the fire breaks the silence.

Outside, the wind whips through the treetops, carrying the wail of a frantic beast. On the bunk, deathly still, Pooch takes short, shallow breaths. Turning his head to the side, his eyes flutter open, sparkling with an icy glow.

~*~

Carrying a pack, Fenimore crunches a new path in the freshly fallen snow as he snowshoes away from the outpost. Pausing to listen to the sporadic shrieks carried on the wind, the trapper looks to his backtrail and then to the snow-covered forest ahead. Guardedly, he lowers his protective goggles. Taking the metal mask out of the pack, he puts it over his face. Rifle held ready across his chest, he continues on, scanning the stretch of trackless snow before him.

XVI

Glowing coals crackle in the hearth, letting off tiny wisps of lingering smoke. The only other illumination in the room comes from gaps in the wooden window shutters and around the front door. Banging open suddenly, the door swings inward, jolting the sleeping men into a mad scramble for their weapons.

A blinding muzzle-flash is followed by the acrid smell of burnt gunpowder. Ducking for cover, someone hollers, *"Who's out there…?!?"* As the smoke settles, the pack-laden trapper steps to the doorway and stands in silhouette.

Recognizing the mask, Quaid yells. "Hold yer fire, boys! He's one of ourn." A match strikes and a lantern is lit, filling the room with a soft glow. Cradling his rifle, Quaid grumbles, "Fenimore, ya nearly got us all t'shootin'… What are ya doin' out there at this hour?"

Stepping inside, the stoic trapper states, "Two of them are gone…" The trapper walks directly toward Wings and pushes past him. He throws back the sick navigator's blanket to reveal an empty bed.

Startled, and then angry, Wings raises his rifle and fans it across the room. "*Who did this?!?*" He studies them, as they stare blankly back. "Where *is* he?" Uneasy looks are exchanged, as everyone slowly backs away from the vacant bunk.

Clearing his throat, Quaid steps up to address the group. "When did this happen? Who took 'im?"

From the back, someone chimes in. "Thank heavens… They did what had to be done."

Fenimore shakes his head as he lays the blanket back down. He turns to the crowd and waits for them to settle before he speaks. "He was not *taken*."

Wings lowers his rifle's aim. "What are you saying…? He was *too sick* to run off…!"

Flight of the Windigo

With an eerie expression, the trapper steps closer to the glow of the lantern. "I followed their trail through the woods for a long distance, until I could not follow anymore."

The room falls deathly silent, until Quaid speaks up. "Where'd they take 'im?" All attention is on the trapper, as they wait for a response. Finally, Quaid repeats, "Dammit Fenimore! Did ya find where they *took* 'im?"

"*He* was not taken. *He* took *them*…"

~*~

An armed search party leaves the outpost and heads into the clinging winter fog. In the lead, Quaid, with Wings at his side, breaks trail for the others following. Bringing up the rear, Fenimore cautiously sniffs the frigid air. They are all unsure about leaving the safety of the trading post…

~*~

At the wagons, Hammer oversees a small group of men that are harnessing horses and loading gear. "Alright, fellas… Da trip ta find da trading post should take ya just a few days, dere and back…" He gives a horse a pat on the shoulder, proceeds to the rear of a wagon and checks inside the empty box. "If dat post is still dere, we need all da food and supplies t'be had." Picking up a rifle, he checks to see that it's loaded. "Dat list I gave ya should cover most ev'ryting dat has to be layed-in fer us t'make it tru dis winter."

Putting the rifle stock to his shoulder and sighting down the barrel, Hammer turns his aim skyward. "Get an estimate on delivery for any items on dat list dat are unavailable and return here as quickly as possible." He turns back to the men and gruffly adds, "No lingerin' wit a pull of da whiskey. *Got it…?*" The men nod in agreement, and Hammer looks up to where the rifle was pointed. He squints, trying to make something out. After a moment, Hammer shrugs it off and puts the rifle back into the wagon. "Dere is a lot of work t'be done here, and dere is somting unknown out dere in dose woods. Sooner yer back, da better."

Walking to the front of the wagons, Hammer watches as the small party climbs aboard. He gives a harness animal a slap on the rump and bids the men farewell. "Good luck to ya, den… See ya in a few days." The wagons roll forward and slowly disappear into the forest. He shivers involuntarily and briefly looks up into the trees again. Pulling his coat tighter around his chest, he shakes off his unease and trudges back to camp.

~*~

As evening sets in, Quaid, Wings, Fenimore and the small group of men sit around a

Flight of the Windigo

warming campfire. With their grim features lit by the fire, they silently stare into the flames. The cold, north wind howls, inspiring a deep feeling of dread in each one of them. It's as if mourning wails of evil spirits are sweeping through the trees, as icy gusts of wind dash down from the starless sky. The flames of the campfire flicker wildly, and a breeze swirls around them before lifting to the treetops and sweeping away over the forest.

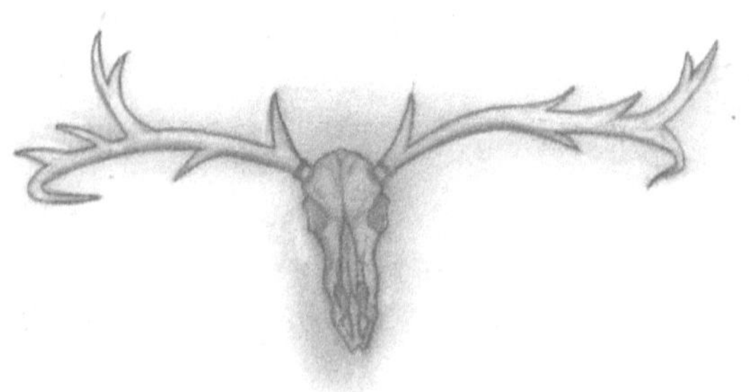

XVII

Dawn brings a clear, bright sky to the northern frontier. Trekking through the woods, Quaid raises a hand to halt the group. Ahead, through the dense forest, they see two stationary wagons with horse teams impatiently stomping their feet. "Hold up here, boys." Quaid warily squats down to observe the situation and motions for those behind him to do the same.

With his rifle tucked under his arm, Wings moves up alongside Quaid. "It might be that crew from S.P.E.C."

"Could be, but they're pointed in the wrong direction."

"Which way *should* they be headed?"

"*Away* from us... Toward the camp."

"Two wagons is kinda small for a replacement team..." Wings considers the group of armed frontiersmen behind him. "I think we've got numbers on our side. We should go over there and meet them."

Pondering this odd situation, Quaid suggests, "Could be that we have more men... Or, it jest might be that they have the element of surprise..."

Following the narrow trail leading to the caravan, Quaid and his group cautiously approach to investigate. Hot breath blowing from their nostrils, the harnessed animals stand alert when they see men approaching. The wagons behind them are void of any person or cargo. Quaid and Wings exchange a wary glance and, impulsively, look up into the trees. Relieved to find no sign of bodies in the canopy, they turn their attention back to the caravan.

A logger climbs up on a wheel hub to peer into the empty wagon box. "Where the heck *is* everyone...?"

Discovering a rifle tucked underneath the driver bench, Quaid shakes his head, perplexed. "Jest abandoned, huh...? Why was there a weapon left behind?" He sniffs the muzzle. "Don't seem to bin fired..." When he levers the action, a live round ejects and lands in the snow at his feet. When Fenimore returns from circling the area, the group turns to face him. Quaid asks, "How many were there?"

The trapper shakes his head and replies, "No sign…"

Eyeing their own path and the rest of the undisturbed forest floor, Wings comments, "They must have walked out."

The trapper shakes his head again. "Two trails lead here. Theirs and ours…"

Skeptical, Wings stares at the stoic man. "Nonsense… They must have walked out the way they came in."

Fenimore shakes his head and replies, "No foot trail… Only the wagon-wheel ruts and horse track leading to here." They get nervous, as Fenimore dons his goggles and mask.

Quaid steps a bit closer to the trapper, speaking low but loud enough for all to hear. "*Windigo…?!?*"

Fenimore silently nods, but Wings scoffs at the idea. "You *must* be kidding!"

Sensing the uncertainty of the men, Quaid climbs up into the second wagon and takes the reins. "Alright, fellas… Some of ya climb into this wagon, and the rest of ya get into the other. We'll turn 'em around and take 'em back to the loggin' camp. Then, we'll burn the whole place to the ground!"

With weapons held ready, some climb aboard Quaid's wagon, and the remainder go to the other one. Wings climbs up next to Quaid. As the team backs up, Wings whispers to him. "Surely, you can't believe some mythical creature just swooped down and plucked these men from the wagons…"

Adjusting the reins, Quaid halts the team and then urges it to turn the wagon and drive forward. "Somethin' sure did…"

"But, we don't know *what* it could have been."

Quaid glances over at the aviator and murmurs, "*Whatever* it was, no wagon driver would leave his animals hitched to an empty wagon in the woods on a winter's eve." Looking ahead, he sniffs the air. "There's a smell hereabout… Ain't sayin' it reeks of death, but it's enough to keep most critters at a distance. See the way these horses stomp as they walk? They gotta fear in 'em, but it ain't of the type that a pack of wolves would cause." Quaid looks over his shoulder to scan the woods. "All I know is, this *whole business* has a stink to it."

Watching the forest for any movement, Wings asks, "Then, why are you sticking with it?"

Quaid slaps the reins again, urging the team forward. "T'was my woman that ate a feller's nose off and attacked yer flyin' partner's arm." Glancing behind, he watches as the other wagon makes its careful turnaround. He shrugs meekly. "Figure it's m'duty t'put 'er down fer 'er wrong-doin's…"

They notice Fenimore walking ahead, studying the wagon party's backtrail. Wearing his frightening metal mask, the trapper turns to look back at them, then walks aside and waves them on. Quaid shakes his head. "If Fenimore don't find any human tracks on the way, these men are gonna lose what little wits they got."

Wings keeps his rifle across his lap, cocked and ready, while Quaid slaps the reins once again driving the wagon in the direction of the logging camp. The aviator looks up through the treetops to see a clear sky and then looks forward to the path ahead of them. "Hell… If *this* don't lead us to some answers… I don't know *what* will."

XVIII

The new logging operation is showing signs of progress. Under the direction of S.P.E.C. engineers, men work on the construction of a massive steam-powered sawmill. Components of tubing and boilers, large gears and saw blades, are being assembled. Hammer heads over from camp to inspect the set-up. Scrutinizing the progress of the rebuild, he questions one of the engineers. "When will da mill become operational?"

"We calculate that the mill should be both complete and able to process logs later today."

"Dats good! Get it up and runnin', and have crews start da milling as soon as possible. Run it tru da night..." As a bone-chilling wind whistles through the treetops, Hammer pauses to gaze upward. "We are already b'hind schedule and need ta make up for da lost time."

~*~

The two wagons move at a slow pace through the snow. Quaid urges the lead wagon's nervous team steadily onward. The second wagon is close behind. Its passengers sit in deathly silence, cradling their rifles while scanning the woods.

Except for the crunching of snow and the creaking of the wagons, the forest is quiet. Suddenly, a gust of wind races through the trees, and a loud shriek, followed by an explosion, breaks the peace. When Quaid hastily pulls up on the reins to halt the wagon team, they all sit listening in apprehension. Then, a forceful breeze, carrying the sound of tree limbs ripping apart, moves past them, and panic spreads through the group. Quaid whispers to Wings. "What the *hell* is *that?!?*"

Squinting in the direction of the horrible sounds, Wings puts a hand up to hush Quaid. "It has to be that S.P.E.C. crew." Perking his ear to the distance, he continues, "They must have the sawmill up and running."

As everyone sits motionless, Quaid looks to the rifle tucked between his knees. "Sounds to me like the flesh-eatin' monster we're after..."

"No… That's the sound of technology."

The frontiersman listens intently another moment and then turns to the men behind him. "Stand ready. Tell 'em others that we're nearin' the campsite." To urge the horses forward, he gives the reins a light snap, followed by another more motivating smack. After glancing at his rifle again, he looks to the aviator on the bench beside him. "The *sound of technology,* ya say…? Ahh, I ain't never had much use fer it."

~*~

The steam-powered lumber mill belches great clouds of vapor, as cut timber, stripped of its branches, is fed in to be sawn into planks. Pleased with the operation, Hammer strolls back toward the main camp. He pauses to investigate the treetops again and gets a shiver when an unusual updraft of cool air sways the branches.

The distinct sound of approaching wagons comes from the same direction as the resupply crew went a few days prior. Hammer does a quick mental calculation of the time they were gone and becomes anxious. When the wagons come into view, he draws a handgun from his coat pocket and blocks their path. As the company wagons draw nearer, Hammer notices that the armed men aboard them are not his. He stands firm, cocks his gun and hollers to the drivers. "You, dere...! *Hold!*"

Prepared to fight, the men on the wagon first study the man blocking their way and then notice the logging operation. Each of them readies their weapons for the imminent clash. Hammer lifts his pistol, aims it toward the first wagon and hollers, "Identify yourselves. Why're you comin' along 'ere in our comp'ny-owned property?"

Holding his rifle across his lap, Wings scoots forward on the bench and speaks to Quaid. "What's this? A *holdup...?*"

Bringing the lead wagon to a stop, Quaid grips the reins loosely and places a hand on his rifle. The men from the back of the wagon climb down and spread out across the snowy trail, nearly encircling Hammer. The brawny mechanic quickly sizes them up and asks, "Where are da men from dem wagons?" When Quaid sets the reins aside and lifts his rifle to his lap, Hammer raises the aim of his gun at him. "Where be my men, and what's yer business 'ere?

"We come to shut this camp down."

Eyeing the guns directed at him, Hammer inquires, "And, why is dat?"

Quaid looks around guardedly, and then moves his gaze to the treetops. "We need you 'nd yer workers to step aside. This place has an infestation of evil spirits, and we mean to burn it to the ground."

Hammer points his pistol skyward and pulls the trigger. The gunshot cracks through the cold air, and a cloud of smoke wisps away on the breeze. Hammer cocks his weapon again, takes a wide stance and declares, "We'll not step aside for any superstitious radicals."

The gunshot draws attention. Men at the camp gather weapons and make their way to the confrontation. On edge, everyone by the wagons brandishes his gun, ready to engage.

Standing in the forward wagon, Wings hollers, *"Now, hold on here!!"* With his rifle pointed skyward, Wings jumps down and pushes his way past several men to get to Hammer. Noticing that Wings is dressed differently from the others, the mechanic queries, "Who might *you* be?"

"I'm one of the aerial scouts sent here to represent the Kishwaukee Valley Logging Company."

Hammer lowers his pistol a bit and bluntly asks, "What's going on here? And, who are dese men you brought?"

"These men are from a trading post to the south of here. They have a firm belief that this area is cursed by an evil spirit."

Hammer shakes his head. "We've seen no such ting."

Surprised, Wings looks behind at Quaid in the wagon, who merely shrugs. He turns back to Hammer and declares, "Less than a month ago, I was here on my initial scouting trip. I reported that everyone was missing."

Hammer eyes the nervous crowd and lowers his gun. "Dis operation has bin re-established, and we are taking over."

Looking to the sizable group arriving from the camp, Wings takes a deep breath. "Less than a week ago, my partner was attacked in this very place..."

XIX

"Rubbish…" Hammer snorts at the notion of ghost stories. "We've seen nutting of da sort."

Moving closer, Wings speaks in a low, serious tone. "You can't *possibly* understand what *terrible* things we've seen *or* what *might be out there*." Realizing that his warning is having little effect, Wings asks, "How long have you been here?"

"Justa few days…"

The aviator looks past Hammer to the group of armed men gathering behind him, and then to the line of tents. "You've seen *nothing* around this camp that might be considered… *unusual*…?"

"Like what…?"

Flight of the Windigo

"Parts of bodies…?"

Raising an eyebrow, Hammer replies, "No… Not hide nor hair." He looks beyond the pilot to the wagons, studying the men that are watching him. Distracted, he sniffs the air. "Are you da flyer belonging to dat machine yonder wit da busted boiler?"

Wings nods. "I am. We arrived last week."

"Who is *we?*"

"My partner and I. We brought supplies."

Hammer looks to each of the men directly behind Wings. "Which one is your pa'tner?"

"He was injured. And, … He's disappeared."

Hammer nods skeptically. "And what of the food stores you were to bring for us?"

"We stashed them in the tent at the center of the camp."

"Well, it seems dat *dey* have disappeared, as well. Perhaps your pa'tner found dat elsewhere dere would be better profit to be made with da food supplies?"

Bristling at the accusation, Wings grips his rifle with both hands. "We're *looking* for my *partner*. And, for a few other men who disappeared with him…"

As more workers from the camp gather behind Hammer, the confrontation gradually shifts to their advantage. The mechanic takes note of this and addresses the visitors accusatorily. "You come *uninvited* to dis place. I ask again… *Where* are da men who *drove dose wagons?"*

Noticing the attempt to rile the crowd, Quaid interjects. "We *found* these wagons *unattended. Everyone* was *gone."*

Evans pushes past several men to be at Hammer's side. Quickly assessing the situation, she looks to Quaid and asks, "Exactly where did you find the wagons?"

Surprised to see a woman in the mix, Quaid clears his throat before snidely answering, "We found 'em in the woods."

Tired of all the back and forth, Hammer raises his pistol, cocks it, and directs it at Quaid. "Have your men trow down deir weapons and surrender demselves to us. If my men are not revealed fortwit, you will be tried for deir murder."

Each opposing faction stands its ground, as the tension escalates. Taking a quick headcount, Quaid tucks his rifle to his shoulder and remarks, "We will *not* go to trial for something we *haven't done."*

Keeping the barrel of his rifle pointed skyward, Wings addresses both sides of the dispute. "Everybody… *Hold it!* We're on the *same side.* We shouldn't be fighting each other."

Flight of the Windigo

Trying to keep a cool head, as well, Evans steps forward. Lifting her hands in the air, she asks, "Why are you here? Where is our crew?"

From the side of one of the wagons, a logger calls out. "We *need* to burn the Windigo from this place! *Let us pass!*"

Evans looks to Quaid, the others, and then back to Wings. "What is a *Windigo*?"

Holding his mask, Fenimore steps out from behind one of the wagons. "It is *here* in *this place. All around* us. It wants to *shape* and take hold of our feelings of fear and anger, then *control* us to do its bidding."

Mocking Fenimore's ominous tone, Hammer scoffs, "And, *who* da *hell* are you wit your scary little mask?"

The trapper ominously sniffs the air, lowers his goggles over his eyes and lifts the mask to his face. "*There* is Windigo... And, it *waits* for us."

Attempting to de-escalate, Evans shakes her head and pushes Hammer's pistol arm down. "We know *nothing* of this Windigo. Only that the earlier crew has abandoned this camp... We were hired to resume the milling operations here."

From the wagon, Quaid declares, "They never *left* here. And, neither will *you*, if ya don't let us do what we *come* t'do."

Realizing that Evans is the most reasonable, Wings asks, "Didn't the logging company give you our report?"

She glances over to see that Hammer is raising his gun again, apparently intent on shooting someone. "We were given minimal information regarding the unusual circumstances of the abandonment."

Turning his aim to Wings, Hammer shakes his head. "I've had 'nough of all dis talkin'. You put down yer weapons, and da rest of ya can surrender yer firearms, too!"

Tilting his masked features skyward, Fenimore looks to the forest canopy, uttering, "It is here *now…*" A frigid gust of wind sweeps down from the treetops, sending shivers through the crowd. Fenimore draws his knife, raises it high, and points at the camp. "*We must cut out and burn the heart of the Windigo!*"

Suddenly, from beyond the camp, there is a massive explosion, and the lumber mill flies apart in a cloud of hissing steam. Everyone runs for cover, as shrapnel rains down and a fireball rises above the trees.

XX

Hammer stares, dumbfounded, as the exploding mill flings metal projectiles through the air. Hunkered on the ground, Evans tugs at Hammer to join her. "Get *down* you, *dunderhead!* One of those things could cut you in half!"

Confused, Hammer looks at her, feebly muttering, "What *happent?* It was *perfect...*"

"*Get down!!!*"

Finally, she ushers Hammer over to where Wings and Quaid are taking cover behind one of the wagons. When he sees the two men, the mechanic's eyes fill with rage. His lips tremble as angry words tumble from his mouth. "It was da fault of da both of *YOU!!!*

As Hammer advances, Quaid puts his rifle across his chest to protect himself. "Wait a minute, fella…"

Hammer jabs a stout finger at them and bellows loudly, "You *said* dat you were here ta *burn us out…!!*"

Wings protests. "We were with *you* this *whole time.*"

Raging like a man possessed, Hammer knocks the rifle out of Quaid's hands and grabs him by the neck. "Dat mill was a *work of art,* and *you destroyed it!!!*"

"Uuughh… *Wait…*"

Hammer shakes Quaid like a rag doll and then slams him against the wagon. "I'll *kill* you for dis…" He hears the cock of a rifle, as its barrel is pressed against his temple.

"Let him go…"

Hammer realizes that it is the aviator holding the gun, and asks, "You work for *us* 'nd stand wit *dem?*"

"I *know* they had nothing to do with that explosion."

Releasing his grip, Hammer tosses the near-strangled man against the wagon wheel and turns to look at the blazing pile of rubble that once was the steam-powered sawmill. Holding back a sob, the mechanic wipes a tear-glazed eye. "Den, let's *see* what *did*…"

As Quaid desperately gasps for air, Wings picks up the discarded rifle and hands it back. The aviator and Evans exchange a look and then turn to watch Hammer stroll toward the source of the explosion.

~*~

The fire has mostly burned out, and the sawmill is a molten pile of wreckage amidst the shells of a few charred tents. As Hammer circles the smoldering mess, he sees bodies being wrapped in tarps and carried away. "Dem were good men…" Donning goggles and heavy gloves, he makes his way to the boiler at the center of the rubble. Mournfully, he shakes his head, as he kicks steaming bits of debris out of his way.

Evans, Wings and Quaid make their way around the perimeter of the mess. Glancing at them, she sadly murmurs, "This puts us out of business here…"

Quaid picks up a piece of bent tubing and tosses it aside. "Looks to be that way…"

Wings nods his head. "Was this everything?"

She stops to look around, puts her hands on her hips and shakes her head. "We're steam-engineers, not lumberjacks… Whatever the heck happened here just took out our boilers... Our source of power. Without them, we're dead in the water."

Quaid looks over his shoulder and up to the treetops. "Ya plan to pack up and git away from here?"

Rage suddenly flashing in her eyes, she turns Quaid, "Did you have *anything* to do with this?"

He shakes his head. "No, ma'am, it was *not* us..." A chill comes over him and he heaves a breath to chase away the uneasy feeling. "There is something wicked in these woods that is beyond my understanding. Something *evil* in the air."

While Wings scans the destruction, Evans turns to him and asks, "What *was* in that report?"

Ill at ease, the pilot exchanges a knowing look with Quaid and then offers, "I don't know what they *told* you..."

"We were informed that this operation was abandoned and needed to be brought back into production."

Before Wings can respond, the frontiersman interjects. *"There was no mention of the bodies hangin' in the trees?"*

Evans stares at them, not believing what she hears. "What?!? *Bodies in trees...?"* She looks to

Wings for verification and he nods grimly. "Could something like that have slipped their minds?"

Wings turns his gaze skyward. "Whatever it is, I fear I've lost my navigator... a good friend, to it. A few days ago, in this camp, he was attacked. He became very sick and then, while in my care, he went missing..."

Appreciating the pilot's frankness, she asks, "Who are the men you brought here?"

"Mostly out-of-work lumberjacks... A few hunters, and some trappers. We joined up with them at the trading post to the south. They feel the need to destroy the demon in this camp. To get revenge..."

As clusters of men confer, Quaid steps closer to Evans and Wings. "The fellas we brought are what's left. Some of the others disappeared shortly before we left the post."

Evans is skeptical. "*Disappeared...?*"

He nods. "And, they ain't turned up yet."

Suddenly an ear-piercing shriek fills the air, followed by a guttural yell from Hammer. With weapons cocked and ready, everyone rushes in the direction of the outburst.

XXI

Gusts of wind blow steam from busted pipes into the swirling smoke and flames. After being tossed across the rubble, Hammer sits up and then stares through the haze at his attacker. Shaken, he smears blood from his lips into his beard, as he climbs to his feet. The wild conflagration seems to snarl, as the mechanic stands to fight.

"Come on, ya bastard!!!"

As if riding the howling wind, a screaming, madman leaps across the burning debris. Hammer greets his attacker with the end of a copper pipe. "Yer a crazy son 'f a…" With his free hand, he turns a pipe valve, and a jet of hot steam blasts into the chest of his assailant.

Flight of the Windigo

The scalded entity releases a blood-curling shriek and falls to the ground in agony. As men circle round to witness the encounter, Wings instantly recognizes him. "My god… *Pooch?!?*" The aviator rushes forward and crouches down to the man squirming on the ground. "Where you *been,* pard?!?" Despite Pooch's tormented look, Wings cradles him in his arms.

Conscious for a moment, Pooch looks up at his friend and tries his best to force a smile. "I'm sorry, pardner…"

"Me too…"

The navigator expires, as shocked bystanders crowd in. They gasp, as an unexpected burst of steam suddenly erupts from the dead man's torso. The chest cavity caves inward, and water suddenly pools in the place where the heart once was. Wings lowers his gaze and releases his copilot. Staring down at the withered corpse, he murmurs, "Goodbye, my friend.

They all close-in to study the ghastly remains. Wings looks up and mutters, "It hardly looks like him anymore."

Shaking his head, Hammer wipes more blood from his mouth and spits into the snow. "Dat dere *monster* tried to take a *bite* out'a me." The gawking crowd regards him tentatively, as he continues. "I do belief, it was going to *eat* me. It tossed me 'round some to *tenderize* me..."

Fenimore steps through a cloud of steam and lowers his metal mask. "I'm sure of it now. He *was* Windigo..."

Hammer turns to face the trapper. "*Jiminy Creepers...!* How many *are* dere of dese Windigo tingys?"

Fenimore joins the group standing over the navigator. "Many have disappeared... By now, there may be dozens."

Hammer touches his sore chin and rolls his shoulder. "Well, it seems dat a good shot of da steam will put 'em down."

Forming an idea, Quaid mutters, "That could be..."

Evans looks at him. "*What* could be...?

The *steam*..." He scans the smoldering mess and replies, "We came ta burn the evil spirits outta this camp. A Windigo heart must melt to be stopped."

In response, Evans shakes her head. "This is our boiler. Most of this equipment is ruined beyond repair."

A chilling breeze sweeps through the group, as Wings looks to the clearing beyond the camp. "There is a good boiler on my aircraft, if you can fix it."

Flight of the Windigo

The wind rotates above them. Gathering up the smoke from the explosion, it swirls it up into the sky and thrusts it back down into the cold, snow-covered forest.

~*~

Loud metallic clanking emanates from the fire-scorched remnants of the camp's main tent. Armed men stand guard, speculating on what might be going on inside. At the mill site, other men sort through debris, hoping to salvage whatever supplies can be found.

Not far away, Wings and a small crew dismantle the aircraft piece by piece. Quaid observes them while on guard, vigilantly scanning the sky and the trees around them. Eventually, the crew separates the boiler from the body of the flying machine and loads it onto a wagon to be transported to the camp.

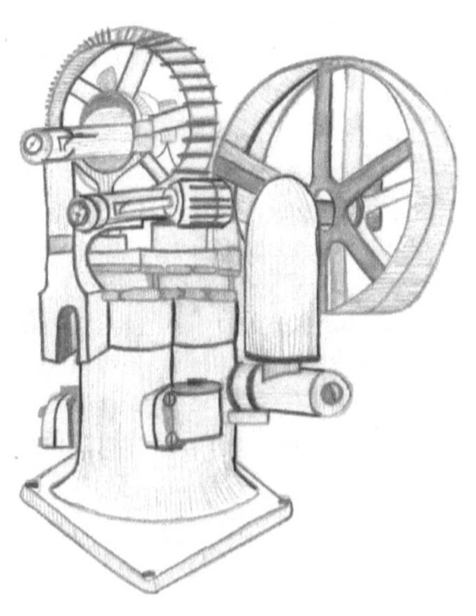

XXII

The evening sky darkens, and lanterns illuminate the large tent at the center of camp. Two guards stand outside the door. As Quaid approaches, they block his path and direct their rifles toward him. "Hold it, there… No one is to disturb them."

Quaid considers the pair of pencil-pushing engineer-types to be ill-suited to guard anything of value. He grumbles, "Let me pass, ya nincompoops."

"They said *not* to be *disturbed*."

"*I'm* the one who *told* them to *post a guard*."

"Well, that's what we're doing… We're guarding."

Disgusted, he raises his voice and calls to those inside. "Hey, fellers…! It's Quaid out here. How's it going with that thing yer buildin'?"

Evans responds. "He's okay, fellas… Let him in." Reluctantly, the guards lower their weapons and step aside. Satisfied, Quaid gives them a tilt of his head and proceeds to peel open the canvas doorway.

Quaid is taken aback by the sight of a wagon carrying a steam-powered monstrosity. Wings is atop the contraption, while Hammer finishes the final repairs to the aircraft boiler. Evans supervises the operation, surrounded by piles of papers, which display plans for a steam-weaponized war-wagon.

Hammer steps from behind a twist of tubing and gauges. Wearing a greasy leather apron and dark goggles, he gawks at the man standing in the doorway. "Shut dat doorway, durn it! You'll let who know's what in here…" Lifting his goggles to his forehead, he looks protectively to where Evans sits.

Shuffling a stack of drawings, she shrugs. "I don't think a canvas door is going to stop much of anything."

Flight of the Windigo

Wings hops down and cleans his hands some on a rag. "Just in time for a test, Quaid…"

The amazed, frontiersman looks over the workspace and appears very much out of his element. Gazing at the machine, he mutters, "What do you plan to test it on?"

Confidently, Hammer bellows, "Da *Windigo ting*, man! We test it on da *Windigo!!*"

With a sly grin, Quaid pulls out his pipe and responds. "Fortunately, at the moment, we have none of those on hand." He lights his pipe, and then peers at Hammer through a curling cloud of smoke. "How 'bout we put this thing t'use on a different sorta cold-hearted character?" Quaid flips the tent-flap and, with a low whistle, waves to someone outside.

Quaid can't help but chuckle at the puzzled expressions of the others in the tent, as a pair of men approach pulling a logging cart in that carries a life-sized snowman. "This should serve the test purpose well. And, building it has kept a few minds off tales of *Windigo*."

Wings is convinced. "Okay…"

Hammer lowers his goggles over his eyes and shrugs. "Fine wit me, it is." He claps his gloved hands together and looks back to the steam-machine. "Heart made of ice, eh?" From the back of the boiler, the mechanic unreels a length of canvas hose with a gun-like nozzle attached to the end of it. Moving toward the snowman, Quaid lifts a hand to stop him.

"How close d'ya think y'll be able t'get to that thing?"

Hammer stops, nods his agreement and takes a few steps back. He looks to where Wings stands next to the controls. "Give me da full power on da valves six and seven."

Wings turns to the controls and twists two of the valves. The machine rumbles to life, and steam hisses through the copper tubing. After seeing the gauges momentarily peak and then settle at a proper reading, Wings turns to Hammer and points at the hose. "Okay, let 'er rip…!" The wagon shudders, the boiler gurgles and tubing whistles, as steam pours though the release valves. Hammer glances at the levels on the gauges, adjusts the nozzle and then tucks the hose firmly under his arm.

Wings steps a safe distance away from the untested machine and notices Quaid start to backpedal, too. The cart sits just inside the doorway, and Hammer waves to the men beside it to move away. "Ya best git clear from dere, 'nless ya want a blast o' hot steam…"

The men by the door scatter, leaving the snow-figure staring blankly at the anxious crowd facing it. Once again, Hammer glances at the gauges. Then, he looks at the nozzle held in his hand. He receives an approving nod from Evans. Taking aim, he braces himself, slowly pulls the trigger, and… nothing happens. Perplexed, he clicks the trigger several more times. "Huh…? What da heck?!?"

Wings moans, "That's just great…", as Quaid quietly curses under his breath.

Hammer gazes at the undamaged snowman staring at him as if to mock his failed attempt. He grumbles to himself, bangs on the nozzle, and clicks the trigger a few more times. Suddenly, a stream of hot vapor erupts and blasts the snowman into icy fragments. Everyone dives away for their own safety. Wings, covered in steaming chips of ice, hunkers down behind a wagon wheel. With his clay pipe dangling from his mouth, Quaid peeks out from behind a wooden crate. Awestruck, Evans grabs for her papers, as the steam continues to pour out, scalding everything in its path.

Eventually, the weapon shuts down, and Hammer observes the results of the test. He sees Quaid over in the corner and smiles at the sight of the man covered in melting snow. Taking his extinguished pipe from his clenched teeth, Quaid examines it. Shaking it dry, he gripes, "Is that how that contraption is s'posed to work?"

Hammer lifts his goggles and then studies the weapon. "It *may* need some adjustin'…"

Looking past what is left of the snowman, Quaid sees the torn strips of canvas that once made up the tent's front door. While the aviator shuts down the last hissing boiler valve, Quaid nods his approval and addresses everyone. "It'll do. When can it be ready to use in the wild?"

Hammer shrugs. "After a few minor adjustments…"

Wings turns away from the boiler. "We should be able to finish it tonight."

As Quaid scrapes wet tobacco out of the bowl of his pipe, he looks at the machine and the ones responsible for it. "Alright… Let's take it out at first light."

XXIII

A hitched team of stout horses stands in front of the large tent, their hind ends tucked just inside the shredded canvas door. Quaid and Wings patiently stand off to one side. The aviator speaks what is on both of their minds. "Do you think we'll be able to find it, let alone destroy it with this thing?"

"You mean, *my woman?*"

"Yeah… Or, whatever has a hold on her…"

"In these woods, drivin' 'round with that enormous contraption, she's gonna be hard t'find."

"You got any ideas on how to lure it here?"

Releasing a puff of smoke from his pipe, Quaid looks around at the men watching, and he murmurs, "Wer standin' amongst the best Windigo bait there is…"

The cold-blooded comment gives Wings a shiver, and he wonders aloud. "Who's gonna *drive* that thing?"

"Damn… I guess, *I* will." Quaid stands watching the uneasy horses paw at the icy ground. "Ya wanna ride up front? I'd feel a whole lot better havin' that rifle of yourn beside me."

The pilot sighs. "Yeah, I'll stay with you and the wagon. Because, if this thing doesn't work, I want my boiler back so I can fly out of here."

Hammer exits the tent and waves. The horses step forward, and the wagon's cargo is revealed. Leaks of steam hiss from joints of copper tubing, making the horses prance and eye the noisy thing behind them. As everyone stands in awe, Hammer bellows, "Stop dat standin' 'round. Git t'yer stations!"

Evans and Hammer climb onto the back of the wagon, near the boiler, and Wings follows Quaid up to the driver's box. Several gun-wielding crew members climb into another wagon. As the procession prepares to leave, those remaining behind in the camp stand watching, conflicted as to which might be the safest option: hunting or being hunted…

~*~

Flight of the Windigo

The weather is calm, as the two wagons make their way into the woods. As the wagons amble down the snowy path, they all watch and wait for signs of Windigo. With a light touch on the reins, Quaid stares ahead, occasionally sniffing the air. From the corner of his eye, Wings watches him and then sniffs as well. He turns to Quaid and whispers, "What do you smell?"

"Nothin'..."

Wings waits a moment to think on his response. He asks, "Then, why do you keep doing it?"

"What...?"

"Smelling the air..."

"Do I...?"

"You've been leading us with your nose like an old hunting dog on the trail of a polecat."

Quaid turns to look at the pilot. "Death has a noticeable stench to it. Cain't describe it, but, when its near, you'll know." Wings sniffs the air again, and Quaid returns his gaze to the harness team and the path ahead. A stiff, icy breeze picks up, rattles through the frozen trees, and blows past them.

~*~

From above, swirling, frigid air swoops down and tears through what's left of the camp. Men scream and dash out of the path of the Windigo.

~*~

Halting the horses, Quaid signals a hush to the wagon behind. When all is still, he tilts an ear to the breeze and strains to listen. Finally, the silence is broken by the distant sound of gunfire. Quaid looks at Wings, and the aviator shrewdly nods. "I hear it…" They both turn to examine the narrow backtrail to the camp. Then, Wings points forward. "There looks to be a place ahead where we can turn." Leaning over the side of the wagon, Wings waves in a circular motion, as he hollers back to the others. "We're turning around…!"

Quaid grumbles, as he slaps the reins, urging the team onward. "Dammit… I should a'figgered…" He reaches a small clearing and turns his team. As he comes around to face the others, Quaid gives several forceful slaps of the reins and yells, "We're goin' back to the camp!!!"

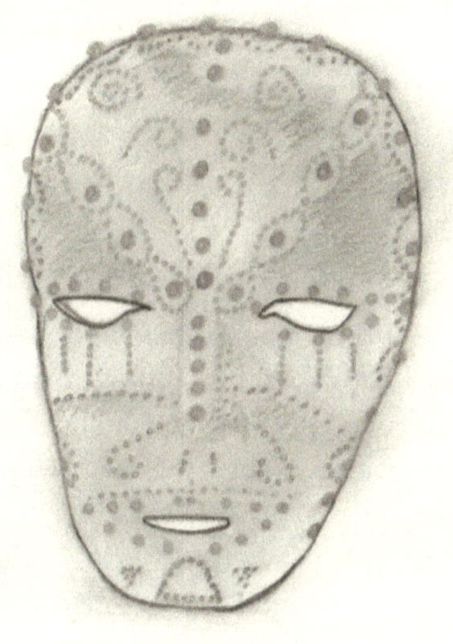

XXIV

Once again, the logging camp, eerily serene after the storm, has been abandoned. As the wagons approach, the draft horses snort apprehensively. Watching for signs of danger, the armed crew keeps the two wagons close together.

Entering the camp, Quaid and Wings exchange worried expressions. The frontiersman breaks the silence and calls out. "Hallo the camp..." As they drive through the ravaged site, they look for any sign of the ones they left behind. Suddenly, they hear rustling coming from one of the broken-down tents.

Quaid halts his team and signals the other wagon to stop. He motions in the direction of the tent. "Hey, flyboy... Better ready that rifle and point it there."

Wings cocks the gun, takes aim and waits. A tense moment later, the tent flap swings open and Fenimore emerges. He holds his knife and is still wearing his protective goggles and mask. His clothing is blood-spattered and torn. The men on the wagons gasp, as the trapper stumbles toward them.

When Wings lowers the aim of his gun, Quaid whispers, "Don't take yer sights off 'im jest yet..." Then, he calls out to the trapper. "Fenimore... What's happened here?"

In reply, the wounded man groans and coughs blood through the mouth of the mask. Quaid tucks the reins aside and climbs down from the wagon. After glancing back to verify that Wings still has his weapon held at the ready, he cautiously advances toward Fenimore. With an open hand out, as if approaching a wild animal, he asks, "Where *is* everyone...? What *happened* here?" Blood dripping from the holes of his mask, the trapper drops to his knees and stares at Quaid. Carefully removing the mask, Quaid reveals a horrific sight. The trapper, missing most of his nose, as well as his lips and chin, is unrecognizable. Gasping, Quaid stares in disbelief. "*This* was from the *Windigo*...?!?"

Suddenly full of life, Fenimore's bared teeth gnash and snap as Quaid stumbles back and falls. Rising to his feet, Fenimore gives a blood-curdling howl that resonates through the ice-crusted trees. In an instant, he is looming over Quaid, ready to attack. A gun fires, but the bullet that rips through the possessed man has no effect.

Wings levers his rifle and fires several more times, but Fenimore reacts as if they are mere distractions. The aviator calls out, "Dammit! *Do* something… *Somebody…!!!*"

Behind Wings, the steam weapon suddenly whistles and hisses, belching clouds of steam. Evans gives the lines full juice, as Hammer, with the hose nozzle held securely under his arm, steps out from behind the wagon.

Before the crazed trapper can continue his attack, a blast of steam fires from the hose. On the ground, tucked into a ball, Quaid covers his face, as Fenimore receives the full brunt of the weapon. The force pushes Fenimore backward and, like a net, one of the few tents still standing catches him. Braced in a wide stance, Hammer continues the spray at full pressure, while Fenimore writhing in agony, is completely overwhelmed by a deadly cloud of steam.

Flight of the Windigo

The weapon finally throttles back, and Hammer releases the trigger. As a hot mist continues to trickle out of the nozzle, he peers toward the cloud of steam enveloping the tent. Keeping safely behind Hammer, men from the other wagon move forward with their weapons drawn.

Still in the wagon box, Wings reloads his rifle and calls out to Quaid. *"You still alive…?"* The frontiersman rolls over, shakes hot droplets of water from his fur coat and sits upright. He turns to stare at the tent, where the cloud of steam drifts away from the trapper's scalded body. Quaid climbs to his feet and moves over to Hammer. "Durnit… I've known that man, Fenimore, for many a year. N'er thought it would come to this."

While steam lifts off the body, Hammer warily nods. "Well, I n'er t'ought I'd be blastin' folks wit a hot-water gun…"

Rifle loaded and ready, Wings asks, "Are we clear…?"

Quaid glances back at him, and then follows Hammer. As they step closer to inspect Fenimore, Quaid self-consciously sniffs the air. Reverently, he folds his hands and bows his head. "Sorry t'see ya go like this, ol' friend."

Behind them, the steam machine continues to run, humming at low throttle. Evans calls to them. "Should we shut it down, or stoke it up?"

Quaid turns to face the men observing and then looks to the weapon. He hollers back at her, "Bring it up to full power. We got some huntin' t'do!"

Hammer looks down at the nozzle in his hand, pulls a length of hose over his shoulder and nods. "Yaugh... We got ta find dat ting, before it comes and gits us all..."

~*~

The men spend the rest of the day searching for others possessed by the Windigo. When a battered and bloody man rushes at them with a crazy sense of urgency, Hammer blasts him without a second thought. As with Pooch and Fenimore, the man shrivels in agony, melting from within.

The bodies stack up, and with the steam weapon stoked and at the ready, the S.P.E.C. crew moves from tent to tent, tearing apart what little remains of the camp. More possessed individuals are dealt deathly blasts of steam, and, eventually, what was once a thriving operation is completely demolished.

XXV

Huddled close together, the survivors sit around a campfire. The soaring flames light up their faces and cast a flickering, orange glow on the wagon-mounted weapon behind them. Evans blows into her mitts to warm her hands, and her glasses steam up as she looks to the others. "How long are we going to stick around here?"

"'Til dey're all gone, I guess..." Then, Hammer glances over to where Quaid sits staring into the fire.

Evans looks from her partner to Quaid and then to the aviator. "How many do you think are left?"

Uncertain, Wings looks at her and then lowers his gaze. "Hard to tell… The ones we've found have been easy pickin's."

Quaid turns from the flames and sighs, as he studies their faces. "It won't be as easy with *her*…"

The haunting comment catches the lone female in the group by surprise. "*Her*…? Who is she?"

The frontiersman looks around and then at the engineer. "There's still one out there who's much stronger than the rest. The *Windigo* took her first as its host and she's the one we need to eliminate to put a stop to all this."

While the fire crackles, there is an eerie silence amongst the group. Eventually, Hammer asks, "What 'bout all dese ot'ers runnin' 'bout tryin' ta eat our faces?"

"The rest are jest weak minions. Without their leader, they'll go to their grave easily."

Unsure about it, Wings looks across the flames to Quaid. When their gazes meet, he comments, "So you're the expert on all things Windigo now?"

"I'm the only one left 'round here who knows."

Momentarily, the two lock gazes, each feeling the heavy loss of someone close. Wings is the first to speak. "It was *your* woman who attacked my navigator."

"*She* was my *wife,* and *Fenimore* was my *friend,* so they meant just as much ta me as *yer* fella was ta *you!*"

Sensing that intense emotions are beginning to escalate, Evans leans forward and puts her hands out for them to stop. "Easy there, boys… We've all lost people in this." With a nod, Wings looks away and stares into the darkness. Evans adds, "We all need to concentrate on our common objective. If she is the strongest, and if stopping her will break the control she has over the others, we need to find her first."

Hammer stirs the fire's embers and adds another log. "Easier said dan done…"

Evans looks to her partner. "How's that?"

Hammer turns to her and replies. "For da past few days, we've bin blastin' dem dat were from our crew a sennight ago. We ain't seen hide nor hair of dis woman who is supposedly at da core of all dis evil."

Quaid takes the pipe from his mouth. "She's around…"

Evans questions, "How did this woman become the source of all this?"

Darting his eyes to each of them, Quaid smooths the whiskers around his mouth and replies. "She crossed the path of a Windigo."

They stare at him, as if he has completely lost his mind. Hammer grumbles, "Sounds like an olt wife's tale to me."

"Ya've seen the results…"

"Well, where is she *now*, den?"

"At our first show of weakness, she'll be upon us. Swoopin' down from the treetops like a winged devil."

Wing's eyes light up. *"Winged devil…?"* Everyone turns to him, waiting for more. Wings looks up at them and exclaims, "We need to fight this evil spirit with wings of our own!"

~*~

The horse drawn wagon carrying the weapon sits at the edge of the clearing. Everyone gathers around the aircraft, which has been gutted of its boiler. Wings circles its remains. He inspects the intact canvas-covered wings and fuselage, mentally forming a plan for renovation.

Quaid addresses the aviator. "What's the *point* of this?"

Mystified, Evans and Hammer exchange a look of concern, as Wings peeks under where the engine was mounted. The mechanic grumbles, "We don't have da spare parts ta equip anot'er engine."

Flight of the Windigo

Wings steps back a few paces and squints at his stripped-down flying machine. He murmurs aloud. "You don't *need* an engine to fly…"

Tugging at his beard, Hammer offers, "It sure *helps*…"

Skeptical, Quaid scans the clear sky and looks back to the aviator. "Ya gonna rope the wind 'n ride it that a'way?"

Wings, turning to address the curious onlookers, states, "It's *all* in the *horsepower*."

Hammer guffaws. "*Horsepower…?*" He looks back at the team hitched to the wagon. "Good luck getting one of dem bone-headed tings hitched up ta *dat…!*"

As the others scoff at the pilot's idea, Evans silently calculates while studying the team of horses. "Wait a minute… He may be onto something."

Tapping the stem of his pipe on his teeth, Quaid mutters, "Gol' damn… You'd have a *winged Pegasus*."

Still confused, Hammer reacts gruffly. "You plan ta put dem wings on a *horse?!?*"

Disappointed, Evans shakes her head. "*No, you dope…!*" She takes off her glasses, wipes them and puts them back on. "The horses *provide the power* to *lift* the aircraft."

As the others begin to understand his plan, Wings faces the group. "That's right. I'll need some time to rig it up, but it could work." Evans steps around the aircraft for a closer look. She touches the fabric-covered wooden ribs and runs her hand over the leading edge of the wing.

Nodding, she works the proposal through in her head. "To get the lift, you'll need a long, clear run. No trees…"

"There's a lake not far from here, where all this started," As they turn to him, Quaid casually sucks on his pipe and lets out a drifting swirl of smoke. Pointing over his shoulder with the stem of his pipe, he shrugs. "*Could* be the very spot to finally *end* this thing…"

XXVI

Traversing the ravaged logging camp, the horse-drawn steam wagon tows the boilerless aircraft. With both wings removed and fastened to the sides to facilitate passage through the trees, the fuselage skids through the snow. Quaid drives the wagon, with Hammer and Evans in the back, ready to use the steam-weapon if needed.

Riding in the aircraft, Wings looks out from the cockpit, mentally scheming how he will turn his plane into a glider. Peering back over his shoulder, he sees the rest of the group following in another wagon.

Reaching the scorched headquarters, Hammer hollers for Quaid to halt the procession. After jumping to the ground, he kicks through piles of debris. Gazing over his shoulder, he calls to Evans. "I'm going to gat'er up whatever tools I can find. Is dere anyt'ing *you* need?"

She peers out over the rubble and shrugs. "I suppose, anything you can find that's usable could be worthwhile."

Hammer gestures to the engineers, and they jump out of their wagon to help him scour the area. "Anyt'ing dat ain't burnt to a crisp, we'll set aside ta use."

Prepared to wait, Quaid takes out his pipe, loads it and tilts his head up to scan the treetops. Glancing back to Evans, he warns, "Whatever ya need to gather here, be quick about it. We should leave this place b'fore nightfall."

~*~

On the shore of the frozen lake, the horses rest nervously, tied to a hitch line strung between the wagons. Everyone keeps to the shelter of the trees, gathering close to the warmth of a campfire, as the sun drops below the horizon.

Chilling gusts of wind whip across the lake and sweep into the forest, causing the trees to ominously rattle and creak. As they sit around the fire, some shiver anxiously, with eyes darting to and fro, while others sit motionless, eyes locked in empty stares. Weapons are held close, as blasts of icy wind lay the flames sideways. Quaid cautions them. "You'd best relax... That wind'll be blowin' all night..."

From the darkness, Hammer steps into the light. "Guards will be switch't out e'ery hour."

The light creates deep shadows on Hammer's features and Quaid asks, "What about the weapon?"

"I have men guarding it, and dey'll be keeping da boiler at a simmer, in case we need it in a hurry."

"Will that thing hold through the night?"

Then, Evans steps in. Looking around, she assesses the anxious faces of the group. "*I'm* more concerned about *us* holding up..." Her stare lingers on Wings, seated by himself. "The plane is all set. You ready to do your thing tomorrow?"

He nods solemnly. "You do yours, and I'll do mine..."

As Hammer takes a knee to throw another piece of wood on the fire, Evans addresses the group. "Let's all get some sleep. We have a big day tomorrow..."

XXVII

While Quaid adjusts the team's harness, Hammer walks over and leans against the front wheel of the wagon. The mechanic is silent as he watches the work. When Quaid finishes his task, he asks, "What's on yer mind?"

"Took a headcount, and dare are *t'ree men* missing."

"S'pose they run-off?"

Shaking his head, Hammer casts his gaze to the treetops. "Naw, mostly just disappeared..."

Quaid takes out his pipe and lights it. He inspects the rig and lets out a puff of smoke. "No tracks to be found?"

"None dat are on da ground..."

Quaid tilts his head skyward and quickly looks away. "Damn… Ever'one know 'bout it already?"

"Not yet…"

"Keep it to yerself. Spread the word that they split off to the south to scout…"

After glancing at the small group by the campfire, Hammer lowers his gaze. "No one will believe it…"

Moving closer, Quaid takes his pipe from the clutches of his teeth and hisses. "These men are near *paralyzed* with fright. We don't have much of a choice, if'n we're to keep 'em from bein' completely useless."

As men pack-up the camp, Hammer glances to the treetops again. Then, he looks back at Quaid. "So… We just leave dem up dere in da trees, as if nothing happened?"

"If any of us make it through this damned ordeal alive, we'll come back 'nd bury 'em proper. Cain't do much for diggin' graves till the thaw anyhow."

~*~

The steam wagon emerges from the woods at the edge of the lake. Urging the horses onto the snow-covered ice, Quaid looks back at the airplane in tow and the meager support crew in the wagon trailing behind. He waves for them to keep up and then gives another slap of the reins. Quaid peers over the side of the wagon and notices how the narrow, iron-rimmed wheels cut cleanly through the drifts of snow. The surface of the lake holds firm, groaning under the heavy weight of the horses and wagons. All are on high alert, dreading the thought of breaking through the ice.

Nearing the middle of the lake, Quaid halts his team, scans around, and puts a hand up to stop the ones following. Ahead, in the fresh snow, is an unusual trail that reminds him of the one he and his woman encountered just weeks earlier. He loops the reins around the brake handle and hops down from the driver's box. Standing knee-deep in the snow, Quaid sweeps his long hair back and puts his ear to the wind. The only sounds are the wind through the trees and the creaking of the ice beneath them.

From the rear of the wagon, Evans calls out to Quaid. "What is it...? Did you find something?"

Staring down at the familiar track in the snow, Quaid feels a sensation of dread. He sniffs the air, looks back at the others and replies, "I've seen a trail like this once b'fore."

Hammer hops down from the wagon and plows his way through the deep snow. "What kind uf trail is it?"

Flight of the Windigo

Quaid puts out his hand, gesturing for him to stay back. "It's time… We better stoke up that boiler."

With a cautious nod, Hammer returns to join Evans and begin preparations. Shuffling through the heavy snow, Quaid backpedals past them. Keeping his eyes locked on the mysterious trail, he follows the towline and reaches where Wings is climbing out of the aircraft. "Prepared to do this?"

"I'll get things set up right now."

"Ya really think this might work?"

With a nervous grin, the pilot offers a feeble thumbs-up. "Affirmative…" He swings one of the wings around and begins attaching it to the fuselage.

Quaid watches the intricate reassembly process, then takes a step closer and steadies one of the wobbly wing struts. When the aviator nods his appreciation, Quaid quietly mutters, "I'm sorry 'bout yer friend."

Wings stops what he's doing. "Thanks… Yours, too."

With no further words to express his feelings, and seeing that the reassembly is almost complete, Quaid heads back to the steam wagon. Wings yells, "Quaid…!" The frontiersman halts in his tracks and looks back, as Wings continues. "Good luck! Hope to see you on the other side."

A smile breaks behind Quaid's overhanging moustache. He takes the pipe from his mouth, blows out a puff of smoke, and raises it to his brow in salute. After checking on the progress of powering-up the steam weapon, he makes his way to the other wagon and gives some final instructions to the armed crew.

XXVIII

As the wagons move forward to cross the path of the Windigo, a fierce, northerly gale transforms the weather. Howling gusts of wind forcefully race over the treetops and, like an upturned whirlpool, circle the frozen lake. After tapping the tobacco from the bowl, Quaid tucks his pipe into his pocket. Peering at the swirling clouds, he flicks the reins, urging the team into a trot.

In the back of the wagon, Hammer and Evans stoke the boiler as steam pours through the valves and twisted tubing. Behind them, the glider lightly bounces along. The taut towline lifts the nose of the aircraft up. Another slap of the reins coaxes the horses to running speed, and the glider lifts off.

As the horses gallop across the lake, snow churns through the spokes of the wagon's wheels. The whipping wind screams, lifting Quaid's fur cap off and standing his long hair on end. He looks behind to see the glider rising into view above the wagon, gaining altitude as gusts of wind lift the wings.

Behind them, the crew wagon charges in pursuit. Suddenly, a blast of icy wind tosses it aside like a plaything, sending it skittering across the lake. The iron-rimmed wheels cut into the surface of the lake, sending chips of ice into the air. A rough patch of ice, hidden by the snow, snaps one of the wheels off, pitching the wagon and its occupants over. Detached from the horse team, the wagon flips repeatedly across the surface of the lake.

High above, Wings deftly maneuvers the aircraft, banking in a wide arc to peer down at the toppled wagon and the panicked horses. With taut features and an intense gaze, he declares, "This is it… Now or never!" Working the ailerons, Wings pitches the plane into a tighter turn and uses the gusts of wind to lift it even higher.

The wagon carrying the steam weapon charges onward. Over his shoulder, Quaid sees the wreckage of the crew wagon, and he curses under his breath. Slapping the reins, he keeps the horses at a steady clip and hollers back to the ones tending the boiler. "Let 'er rip! Now's the time!!!"

Steam pours from the joints of the stoked-up machine, as Hammer climbs out and up to the top of the speeding wagon. At the rear of the rig, Evans reaches out to him, passing the steam nozzle and hose. She watches him brace for the fight. Turning his gaze skyward, Hammer observes the glider as it zips along at the end of the tether line, slicing through the raging windstorm.

Nearing the edge of the lake, Quaid looks to the trees ahead, then back to the wrecked support wagon and then up at the airplane. The strong winds blow his beard against his face, blocking his vision as he turns to look forward. He pushes it down under his chin and shouts, *"Yeooweee!!!"* Pulling hard at one set of reins, he guides the horses in a tight turn that skids the wheels across the surface of the lake. With the sudden turn, the glider slingshots around, gaining altitude.

As Wings works the controls to adjust for the sudden increase in speed, the aircraft's tether creaks under the strain. He braces himself, as the jerk of the line brings the glider's nose around to follow the speeding wagon. Rope taut, the glider rises like a kite in a storm, while all around him, the icy wind swirls with a supernatural frenzy.

The wagon charges ahead at full tilt, pulling the glider higher. Stabilized on the top of the wagon, Hammer stands with the nozzle held ready. The threatening wind continues to swirl, as if intending to consume both the wagon and the plane.

Matching the wagon's speed, the malevolent windstorm flows down the tether line. Hammer's eyes fill with terror, as the storm bears down. Bracing himself, he unleashes a blast of steam. Aiming the hot spray upward, Hammer lets loose the contents of the boiler on the ferocious windstorm.

When the steady blast of steam is suddenly cut short, Quaid hollers, "What's goin' on back there? Why'd ya stop?"

Still braced atop the speeding wagon, Hammer is mystified. "I tink I *got* it… At least, I *tink* I did!"

High above them, the violent winds continue to howl as the wagon charges across the lake. Nearly blinded by the swirling snow, both men look up. Then, Quaid turns forward and whips the reins on the tired horses. "The *hell* ya did...!"

Above, the glider jerks violently against the tether line. The storm's relentless hold rocks the plane through the air. Wings attempts to control the aircraft one-handed, while he fires his rifle using the other.

In the skies above the wagon, the wind tears ferociously at the plane and lone aviator. Wings swings his rifle barrel out from the cockpit and fires indiscriminately. Sensing his end is near, he screams at the top of his lungs. *"Eat lead, Windigo...! Curse you for taking my friend!!"*

He releases his grip from the useless controls and rapidly levers the rifle, firing again and again. One of his shots unintentionally grazes the tether rope, and it begins to unravel. Shooting madly, Wings hollers into the raging windstorm. *"Give me your best, you son-of-a-bitch!!!"*

When the rope suddenly snaps, the glider whips swiftly upward, veering over the expanse of lake and toward the trees. Wings finally shoots his last round and tucks his rifle back inside the cockpit. At the mercy of the wind, he desperately tries to regain control of the aircraft.

XXIX

From the wagon, Hammer sees the aircraft get violently ripped from its tether and sucked higher into the storm. He hollers to Quaid. "We lost da glider...!!!" Quaid looks over his shoulder to the weapon and then to the clouds. Surprisingly, the sky suddenly clears and, high above the trees along the shoreline, they can see the glider with the loose end of the rope trailing behind it.

Quaid yells to Hammer. "Look there! I think we *got* it..." Soaring through the blue sky, banking for a return to the lake, the glider is suddenly confronted by a blasting downdraft that breaks the wings and smashes the fragile craft into the trees. Quaid pulls back on the reins, and the exhausted horses blow for air as the wagon slows.

Quaid looks all around, sniffing the air. Uncertain, Hammer braces himself and aims the hose nozzle skyward. Then, the wary mechanic lowers it and mutters, "Where'd it go? Maybe it's gone from dis place?"

Screaming across the treetops, the windstorm returns as quickly as it left. Catching the smell of death in the air this time, Quaid slaps the reins mercilessly on the backs of the exhausted team of horses. "*Hell, no…!* It's comin' fer *us* now!!!"

The wind smashes, broadside, into the wagon, nearly flipping it over. Knocked from his position, Hammer falls onto the steam weapon and holds tight. Protected from the hot boiler by his heavy clothing, the mechanic repositions himself and looks ahead to the shoreline. At the edge of the forest, he spots the path to the logging camp. "Head for dem trees… It might be our only chance!!!"

Frantically driving the wagon across the ice, Quaid flees for their lives. He slaps the reins repeatedly and calls back to the others. "*Hold on, back there!*" Above them, the storm swirls around, gaining power as it pursues them toward the shore.

Flight of the Windigo

The wagon reaches the shoreline, bounces over the steep embankment, and heads for the pathway through the woods. Back on his feet, Hammer holds the steam nozzle high, opens it wide, and sprays steam in every direction. As the wind swirls around him, he defiantly bellows to Quaid up front. *"Da ting is on us now!"* Between blasts he hollers, "Get us *away* from here!"

Slapping the reins furiously, Quaid yells back to him. "Hold on, I'm takin' us back to the camp!"

Hammer continues to blast steam skyward, keeping the storm at bay. He shouts to Evans, as she monitors the boiler and adjusts the pressure gauges. "We need more damn steam for dis ting! Keep dat boiler pumping!!!" Evans stays on task, holding tight, as the wagon barrels through the woods at breakneck speed.

~*~

As they enter what remains of the scorched logging camp, Quaid pulls back on the reins to slow the team down. The horses scream in wild protest, straining against the traces. Steam rises from their lathered hides, and pants of steaming breath explode from their flared nostrils. Quaid brings the animals to a halt and Hammer, cutting the spray from the gun, nearly topples from the top of the wagon. He calls to the driver. "Whoa! What's da holt up!?"

Ahead, on the narrow trail through the camp, they are astonished to see the native woman standing in their way.

Hammer exclaims, "Who is dat?!?"

Holding the reins, Quaid stares awestruck. "It's her..."

Peeking around the boiler and seeing Quaid's woman, Evans remarks, "She don't look so tough." She calls to Hammer up top. "We're nearly out of steam! We need to recharge."

Taking aim with the nozzle, Hammer jabs a finger forward and shakes his head. "Dis is *not a good time...*"

Quaid puts aside the reins and lifts his goggles to his forehead., When the possessed woman looks directly at him and summons, Quaid stands. As he starts to climb down from the wagon, Hammer hisses, "Where dit dat woman *come* from? And, where are *you* going, you *bearded ninny?!?*" The mechanic reaches out to grab Quaid, but the frontiersman pulls away and leaps to the ground.

Charmed by the woman, Quaid walks forward, as she beckons him closer. Casually, he drops his weapons and his heavy fur coat, expressing his vulnerability. The icy winds begin to calm, and soon the camp is still. From atop the wagon, Hammer looks down to Evans and mouths a silent command. "Git dat steam pumping... *Now!!!*"

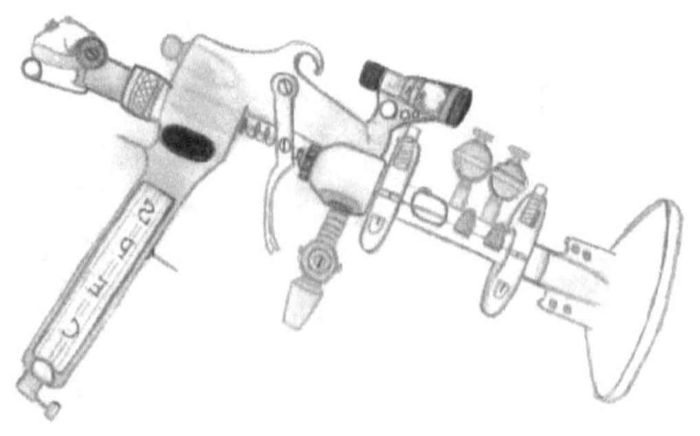

XXX

Quaid approaches the woman, seeing her as she once was. Lost in memories of days gone by, he tenderly reaches out to hold her. She coyly smiles, just as his mitted hand touches her. Suddenly, she transforms from her youthful beauty and former innocence to a hollow-eyed demon with sharp, gnashing teeth. With lightning-fast reflex, Quaid breaks from his trance and grabs a firm hold of the woman. Snapping her jaw ferociously, she lets out a soul-chilling wail. Embracing her tight in his arms, Quaid spins her around to face the steam wagon. Frantically, he yells, "Do it now! Free her *heart* from this thing*!!!*"

The woman, possessed by the demon within, launches into a tornado-like spin. Quaid desperately clings to her, unable to escape the raging vortex. As the whirling dervish whips him round and round, he wails, *"Shooooot nowwww!!!"*

Hammer aims the nozzle of the steam gun, then looks questioningly to Evans. She shakes her head, motioning that she needs another minute to finish recharging the boiler. Hammer looks back to see Quaid spinning at a dizzying speed. Urgently, Hammer pleads, *"Evans…!* We haf'ta make it go *now!* I don't tink he has anot'er *minute…"*

Summoned by the *Windigo,* dark and twisting clouds gather overhead. Strong winds sweep through the treetops, breaking limbs as they pass. The frigid air cracks like thunder, and Quaid is suddenly flung forcefully against a downed tree. Rising into the cyclone, the monster, that once was the woman, lifts from the ground to match the height of Hammer on top of the wagon. She greets him with an ear-piercing scream. With her arms spread wide, she reaches out to pull him into a soul-freezing embrace.

Through the chaos, Hammer faintly hears Evans yell, *"Go time…!! It's ready!!!"* Opening the nozzle, he endures a moment that feels like an eternity, before an explosion of steam unleashes directly toward the *Windigo*. A series of horrifying shrieks fill the air, as the scalding-hot discharge plows into the deathly spectre. The furious winds suddenly explode outward, flinging the camp's wreckage high into the air and stripping bark from trees as far away as the eye can see.

Hammer continues to direct a constant flow of steam toward the wind-creature. Despite the freezing air swirling around him, he sweats profusely. He hears Evans scream, "There isn't much left…" While the demon wails in bitter agony, Evans yells, "*Finish it…!!!*"

Hammer cranks the nozzle fully open and gives the *Windigo* everything the boiler has left. Through clenched teeth, he snarls, "Damnation… I'm givin' dis devil-ting *all we got!!!*" As the steaming spray pours into the swirling mass of icy wind, the ultimate death cry of the Windigo rises to a deafening level. Then, as quickly as they had first formed, the menacing storm clouds mysteriously clear away, and the swirling gusts of icy wind withdraw.

The camp is eerily quiet, as the last trickles of vapor seep from the nozzle of the steam weapon. Atop the wagon, Hammer drops to his knees and heaves an exhausted breath.

Below, Evans hops to the ground and looks up to her partner. Then, her gaze shifts to the clear, blue skies. Meekly, she utters, "Hammer... I think we *did* it."

They look to the wind-swept pathway and see Quaid sitting on the ground. In his arms, he cradles his native wife, now returned to her human form. Oblivious to everything else, the frontiersman gazes lovingly down at her, brushes her dark hair back and holds her firmly to his chest, as life slips away. Quaid heaves his last breath and crumples over.

Approaching the couple warily, Hammer groans feebly. "Hrmmphh..."

Evans adds, "I didn't think the fella had it in him."

Hammer looks over at her. "What is dat?"

She stares at the reunited couple in an eternal embrace. "Caring for anything other than himself."

Hammer shakes his head, glances at the steam nozzle still in his hand and tosses it aside. "When da chips are down, da true self can come out."

~*~

After unhitching the team from the wagon, Hammer hoists Evans onto the bare back of one of the horses. He tosses a set of saddlebags across the other one and leads it alongside. As

Flight of the Windigo

they depart the camp, Evans looks back to where Quaid and the woman sit in a frozen pose of intimacy. "Wait... Don't you think we should bury them? Put them to rest in some way...?"

Hammer sees Quaid's pipe on the ground and reaches down to pick it up. He studies it for a moment, then tosses it over to where the couple sit. "Dey are *already* put ta rest."

As snow flurries begin, Hammer looks up to the swaying treetops and then back at the odd pair on the ground. "Da ground is much too hard for digging. We'll leave dem to melt away wit da spring thaw." He gives the pack animal's lead line a tug, and they break trail through the woods in the snow. With a shiver, Evans turns away from the devastated logging camp and urges her mount to follow after her partner.

As the pair of survivors slowly disappear into the forest, large flakes fall gently over the campsite, slowly erasing it with a blanket of snow. From the north, a westerly wind picks up, howls momentarily and then fades away amongst the treetops.

The End...

<u>Note from Author</u>

Told to me by a friend during my time in film school, the tale of the *Windigo* comes from Native American folklore. We were putting together a story that could satisfy several assignments for class, and eventually we wove them together to create a short film. With a limited budget, but access to state parks such as Devil's Lake in Wisconsin, and other wilderness locales - what better way to make use of the Midwest winter.

In the wild, when put to the ultimate test of survival, the human mind can be a fragile thing. There are multiple tales of frontier people going crazy due to cabin fever or, worse yet, there are stories of people resorting to cannibalism in order to survive a long winter. How did they explain the evil that can possess someone to do terrible acts against himself or others? As anyone who has spent time in the outdoors knows, an incessant wind can drive you crazy…

Hope your trail does not cross the path of the Windigo.

Eric H. Heisner

October 5, 2024

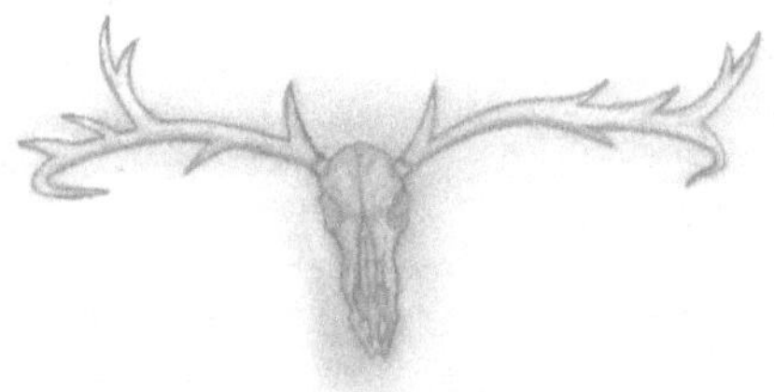

If you enjoyed *Flight of the Windigo*,
read other stories by
Eric H. Heisner

www.leandogproductions.com

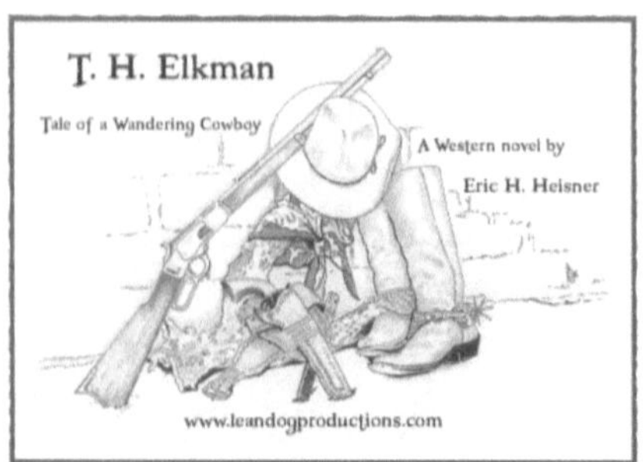

T. H. Elkman
Tale of a Wandering Cowboy
A Western novel by
Eric H. Heisner
www.leandogproductions.com

WEST TO BRAVO
A Western Novel
By Eric H. Heisner
WWW.LEANDOGPRODUCTIONS.COM

Wings of the Pirate
A high-flying Adventure Novel
By Eric H. Heisner
Limited time pre-order at:
www.inkshares.com
illustrations by
Al P. Bringas
www.leandogproductions.com

Eric H. Heisner is an award-winning writer, actor and filmmaker. He is the author of several Western and Adventure novels: *West to Bravo, T.H. Elkman, Africa Tusk, Conch Republic* and *Short Western Tales: Friend of the Devil.* He can be contacted at his website:

www.leandogproductions.com

Adeline Emmalei is a creative artist, student and animal lover. She lives in Austin, Texas.

www.ingramcontent.com/pod-product-compliance
Lightning Source LLC
Chambersburg PA
CBHW021709190726
48289CB00008B/2441